HEIRLOOMS AND HOMICIDE

HEARTS GROVE COZY MYSTERY, BOOK 1

DANIELLE COLLINS

FAIRFIELD PUBLISHING

CONTENTS

With a cup of coffee from *Espresso Yourself* and the town's newspaper tucked neatly under her arm, Henrietta Hewitt entered the front door of H.H. Antiques ready to conquer the world. Or at least her to-do list for the day. There was something to be said about the smell of fresh coffee and the right attitude, at least that was what Henrietta's mother had always said. She hoped that it would prove true because today, she needed to attack a massive list of projects and she could use all the help she could get.

Sepia, a creamy tan Flame Point Siamese, ran across her path, nearly tripping Henrietta with her long tail. "Hey now," Henrietta cautioned. "You don't want me spilling this hot coffee. It would not be a pretty sight."

The cat, now safely across Henrietta's path, sat and stared back at her with inscrutable blue eyes. She sent out a pink tongue, licking away part of her breakfast, no doubt, before turning to jump into the top of the old grandfather clock by way of a wing-backed chair and antique hutch in succession. If they ever sold the clock, Sepia would be forced to find a new roost.

The sound of the tiny silver bells hung at the front door drew Henrietta's attention away from the mischievous cat.

"Hello?" she called out.

"It's just me," a breathless voice replied. Then, through the narrow hallway of the Victorian house-turned-antique shop, Henrietta's assistant and fellow historian appeared.

"Why, Olivia, you're early."

"Is it really that surprising?" the young woman said. Nearing thirty but not looking a day over twenty-five, Olivia wore a flowing, dark green tank top over jean capris. Her boxy, horn-rimmed glasses perched on a petite nose and when she smiled, her pale blue eyes sparkled beneath blunt-cut bangs.

"No. Well, yes," Henrietta said with a shrug.

"I know. I'm usually late." Olivia rolled her eyes at herself and mirrored Henrietta's shrug. "But it's never too late to turn over a new leaf, is it?"

"Liv," Henrietta said, staring her down with what she hoped was an encouraging look. "You do what you need to."

Olivia broke into a shy smile and nodded toward Henrietta's coffee. "Already got a cup?"

"Yes," Henrietta said, sighing and turning to the

counter where the cash register sat between a stack of antique books and a box of odds and ends that still needed cataloging. "It was going to be *a morning* without it."

"I hear that." Olivia deposited her purse beneath the counter and subconsciously pushed her glasses up the bridge of her nose. "Mind if I pop next door?"

The call of *Espresso Yourself* was strong and Henrietta didn't know many who could resist. Having a coffee shop next door was a blessing and a curse.

"No problem. Tell Gina it's on me."

"Oh, you don't have to do that."

Henrietta responded with a look, and Olivia flashed a smile before disappearing back toward the front door.

So much for being on time, Henrietta thought good-naturedly. She'd hired Olivia two months prior and was fairly certain the woman hadn't been on time once, but when it would have bothered her immensely in anyone else, Henrietta found that Olivia was worth the few minutes she missed at the beginning of her shift. She rarely went home on time and often stayed late to hunt down a date for an item or a price from an overseas carrier. Her tardiness was more than made up for by her effectiveness.

Henrietta turned her attention to the yellow legal pad next to the register. She'd started her list last night before going upstairs into the living portion of the house. The list was extensive and possibly a bit too

3

ambitious, but she was willing to give it her best shot before the clock struck six and she turned into a pumpkin. Or, more likely, before her feet turned into miniature pumpkins and she was required to put them up to rest.

The bells rang again, and she called out, "That was fast."

"Miss me that much?" a masculine voice said.

Henrietta looked up into the chocolatey brown depths of Ralph Gershwin's eyes. His bushy eyebrows wagged up and down a few times and he cracked a smile.

"Ralph? What are you doing here this early?"

"Came by to see you," he said, leaning against the counter and peering down at her list. The man made his late fifties look good, though Henrietta tried not to notice.

"And?" she offered, waiting for him to tell her the real reason he was there.

"And..." He looked up at her. "I've got a missing persons case."

Henrietta rolled her eyes heavenward. "Sepia, do you hear that? Ralph's got a case! What *has* he done to deserve such favor?"

"No need to be snarky," he said with a low laugh.

"I know. It's just that..." She huffed out a breath and felt her hands go to her hips. He brought this out in her. "You come in here expecting a different answer, and I just can't give it to you, Ralph."

"You wound me," he said, clutching his hand to his chest.

"If you'd like for me to read you my latest chapter, I'd be more than happy to, but aside from that and your occasional masculine help with lifting heavy objects, I don't think we can afford to be in business together."

"You say it like it would be a bad decision, and I just can't believe that."

"Ralph…" She leveled her gaze at him, willing the full force of her feminine persuasion to convince him. "I will not join your private investigation business."

"Yet."

"What?" She had already turned away to start numbering the items on her list.

"You forgot to add 'yet' to the end of that statement." He stood with his hand out and affected a nasally, almost feminine tone. "Ralph, I will not join your private investigation business—yet."

"I—"

"*Tisk tisk,*" he said with an upheld finger. "Let me tell you more about this case."

She was going to refuse but the bells rang again, and she thought the phrase 'saved by the bell' had never been more appropriate.

"Olivia and I have *much* to do. Good day, Ralph."

He looked wounded, but she knew it was an act. As much as he tormented her, trying to get her to join his father-son private investigation agency, she also counted him as a friend and knew better than to think her declining his offer would stop him.

"Maybe another time," he said, looking at Olivia and winking. She giggled and nodded in an exaggerated way.

They were both insufferable.

"Good day," Henrietta said.

"Bye, Henri," he said with a laugh before turning to leave.

"What did Ralph want?" Olivia asked, setting her coffee down on the counter and brushing her hand through her wind-tossed bob.

"The usual."

"You offered to read him your chapters again, didn't you?"

"So what if I did?" Henrietta said, not looking up from her list prioritization.

"No wonder he left so quickly."

The Blackberry Festival was only a few days away and Henrietta felt confident it was going to be their biggest year yet. Then again, every person in town always thought that *that year* was going to be the best yet. Perhaps it was the pull of festival season, the warm weather and beautiful days, or maybe it was the cute little town buried deep in Washington, but Henrietta was happy to believe the best about each festival season as it came.

"You'll have it, won't you?" Mayor Ricky Lawrence said, his thin hands nervously clenching and unclenching in front of him.

"Of course, Ricky." Henrietta took a moment to move to the window in the mayor's office. It was four stories up in one of the tallest buildings in Heart's Grove, and it afforded a lovely view of the ocean. "Have I ever let you down?"

"What? Oh, no, no, no," he said in his characteristic twittering tone. "It's not so much that as the pressure. Oh, the pressure." While Ricky was something of a visionary, he was a worrier five times over.

He'd checked in with Henrietta at least once a week starting two months before the festival to make sure that she'd contribute her usual item for the silent auction.

"Don't worry," she said, turning back to him. "I'll have something extra special. I've got a few items in mind, actually."

"Care to give me a hint?" he asked, coming to stand next to her at the window. Somehow, the beautiful view didn't seem to distract him as it did her.

"Not yet, but soon." She offered him a confident smile as she picked up her purse from the side chair. "I'm off. You'll be hearing from me soon."

"Shouldn't you already have the item?" he called after her.

Her only response was a raised hand offering a wave.

They went through this dance every year: Ricky worrying about every minute detail of the festival, Henrietta assuring him that she had her part under control, and him asking a thousand questions that she dodged artfully until she was ready to answer them.

A woman's mystery is never to be underestimated, Henrietta remembered her mother saying. It seemed as appropriate in this situation as it did in many other aspects of life.

When she reached her Mini Cooper, she climbed inside and tossed her purse on the seat. She had an auction to get to and if she didn't hurry, she might miss it.

The sound of loud rapping on her passenger window startled her enough to entice a short scream. Ralph's grinning face was enough to turn the scream into a growl. She rolled down the window.

"You know better than to scare a woman who's got her foot on the brake," she said.

"That I do. Your break lights weren't on yet."

She let out a sigh. "They were about to be."

He laughed. "Mind if I tag along?"

"To?"

"The auction you're going to."

She opened her mouth but closed it. How had he known—

"You saw the paper on my desk this morning."

"Bingo." He opened the door and began to slide in, almost sitting on her purse before she yanked it away from him. "Can't get anything past you, Henri."

"I really wish you wouldn't call me that."

His knees hit the dashboard. "Really? Why do you have to drive a clown car?"

Feeling as if his cramped space was punishment enough, she decided to forgive his fright-inducing interruption to her day. "How's the missing person case going?" she asked as she pulled into traffic.

"Thought you weren't interested?"

"I never said that." She narrowly avoided someone pulling into traffic—making Ralph gasp and flinch—before she shot a look his way. "I merely said I wouldn't join your agency."

"Feels like the same thing to me."

"Believe me, it's not."

He tried, and failed, to adjust his position to give himself more room as she turned onto a two-lane highway. If they continued west, they'd end up in Port Angeles, but they weren't going that far.

"Name's Cybil Markham. Young girl, early twenties, black hair, hazel eyes. Apparently, she's run away from home."

"Seems like a case for the police," Henrietta mused.

"Sure, sure." He nodded, knowing full well that Henrietta was right. Ralph had been a police detective for most of his life and, after deciding to retire from the force early, had created a private investigation agency with his son, Scott, a kind, single man in his early thirties. "The parents are from New York—"

"Do they think she's come here?"

"Are you going to let me brief you on this or do you want to keep guessing, Agatha Christie?"

She made a face, and in her silence, Ralph got his answer.

"Her parents, in New York, went to the authorities. They searched her room and found a note saying she was leaving. Since there was a note and she's of age, they really had nothing else to go on."

"So, they hired you to find her. Again, I ask, why here?"

"Apparently," he said, drawing out the word in exasperation, "she purchased a bus ticket from there to here by way of Seattle. That was the end of her trail. They contacted me—found me on the web and emailed me—and the rest you know."

Henrietta couldn't help her smile. Ralph had been bragging about the amazing job his son Scott had done in setting up a website for their agency. While she had to admit that it was a nice site, the pride which Ralph spoke of his presence on 'the web' was more than a little inflated.

"Any leads?"

"Not really," he shifted his weight, groaning. "I've got a few things I'm looking into, but—"

"Don't even think about it," she said, pulling onto a long, paved driveway toward a cliff-side mansion.

"But—"

"Nope." She shot him a sideways glance, and he pursed his lips. "But you can help me search for the perfect item for the Blackberry Festival auction."

"I thought you were already supposed to have that."

"Not you too," she said with exasperation.

They pulled up as close as they could and parked on the grass as an attendant instructed. As they climbed out of the car, Ralph making an over-exaggerated grunt that sounded like "Freedom," Henrietta took in the massive house. It was at least three stories high in a Victorian style and looked to have been newly painted. She assumed they were preparing it for the market after the death of the home's original owner. There were likely a lot of wonderful things to find within its historic walls.

"Let's go!" she said cheerily.

Ralph looked as if he wanted to say something—likely something about her participation in his case—but he closed his mouth and gestured for her to lead the way.

They'd see just how long his silence lasted.

2

———

Climbing the front steps of the Victorian home, Henrietta imagined what the house must have been like before it was modernized. Brushed copper fixtures had no doubt replaced the original wrought iron gas lamps. The front door, now a modernized, boxy design, had taken the place of a crafted door with molding inlays and an antique ringer that made a charming bell noise when the knob was turned. Even the original, thin-width deck boards had been replaced with larger planks and painted over.

While Henrietta hadn't seen the house up close until today, she could imagine all these things with perfect clarity. They would have been standard in most Victorian homes in this area and she felt a pang of sadness at the reality that those things were lost to the way of the modern footprint.

"You look sad," Ralph observed.

"Not so much sad as disappointed."

"Why?" He held the door open for her.

"They've completely modernized this place."

"Likely fixed to sell."

"Yes," she agreed, stepping into the modernized foyer, "but there is a way to preserve history while affecting modern change that preserves the historical accuracy. It merely takes a little creativity. Something their designer certainly lacked." She lightly touched the tip of a modern, metal sculpture in the corner of the entryway. It was large and garish, in her opinion, and had no artistic structure to it. Not like the Victorian era.

"Buy this place and fix it up," Ralph said with a laugh. His neck was craned to take in the ceiling and he missed Henrietta's expression, which she was thankful for. There was no need to tell him she'd considered that very thing not moments ago.

"Welcome to Patton House. We're pleased that you could join us today. Do you need a pamphlet for the auction?"

"I brought mine along," Henrietta said with a smile.

"Delightful," the tall man said. He had thinning gray hair and a smile that said he was paid to be courteous. "We'll begin in twenty minutes in the library. Just that way." He indicated an extremely large hallway that led toward the north wing of the home.

He walked away as another couple entered and began his welcome again.

"What do you do at these things?" Ralph said. He looked out of place in his khaki cargo shorts and knock-off Hawaiian shirt. All he was missing was a fishing hat and he'd fit right in on the deck of a fisherman's boat.

"We observe," she said with raised eyebrows.

"Ah, something I should be good at."

She resisted the barb that came to her almost as easily as breathing and led the way up the wide staircase. It wound around to each floor in turn, but she stepped off on the first. Thankfully, the banister had been preserved in its original form and she admired the scrollwork and rich mahogany coloring of the wood.

"How about this?" Ralph said, holding up the lid to a large, Japanese vase.

"Put it down," she said, racing toward him with hands outreached.

Wide-eyed, Ralph gently returned the ornate lid to its resting place.

"That is an eighteenth century agateware vase. They are enormously expensive."

Ralph's eyes widened even more. "Guess I'll stick to looking, not touching."

"Wise." She spun on her heel and headed for the playroom as indicated in her directory. There were a few children's toys of vintage quality that she'd considered acquiring for the shop. One of them could be suitable for the silent auction, but she'd have to see them in person to make that choice.

"What's this?" Ralph pointed to a colorful box sitting on the table.

She grinned. "That's a jack-in-the-box. Just try it."

"I think I'll pass on this one." He grinned, and she laughed. She would have said the same thing.

Henrietta went back to circling the large room. She guessed that there would have been floor to ceiling wallpaper in this room. It was gone now, replaced with a light seafoam green color. The moldings had all been painted white, giving the room a beachy, airy feel. She liked it, despite the fact that history had been changed to create that feeling.

All around the room were large folding tables that held various artifacts and auction items. Henrietta maneuvered around the tables with a keen eye for anything that would appeal to the various online buyers she often sold to as well as tourists who might grace her shop in the coming months. Christmas would soon be upon them—or so it felt as a business owner—and she always had to be thinking ahead.

"How about this?" Ralph said, pointing to a small box. "It's pretty."

She was about to roll her eyes and comment on Ralph's inexperienced eye when something in the shape and make of the box caught her attention.

"Hmm," she said, the noise drawing a smile from Ralph.

"Don't tell me I *actually* pointed out something you might be interested in. Let the hallelujah chorus play."

"Don't get ahead of yourself." She walked past him and bent over the table, careful not to let the long beads of her necklace hit the table as she did.

The box looked as if it was made from many different types of wood, including burl, which was highly prized. She so badly wanted to pick up the box but knew better than to touch the auction items. One wrong move and she could be paying thousands, or *hundreds* of thousands, of dollars for an item that was damaged.

"What is it?" Ralph asked, leaning down and peering over her shoulder.

"I'm not certain, but it seems to be very old. I think this is a rare treasure, though how rare, I wouldn't know until we'd have a chance to research it. Too bad Olivia isn't here." She shot him a look.

"Sorry I'm not as useful as your assistant."

They grinned at each other just as a gong sounded downstairs.

"It's time for the auction to start. Let's go downstairs. And, Ralph," she said, pausing in the doorway to meet his gaze, "Don't take a paddle unless you're willing to spend a thousand dollars for accidentally using it as a fan."

He nodded. "Noted."

Fortunately, the toy room, as they were calling it, was close to the beginning of the auction. They had only sat through a few previous rooms by the time the small items were brought onto the stand.

Henrietta bid on a metal wind-up toy, winning by fifty dollars ahead of a snooty-looking older man whom Ralph dubbed Mr. Highbrow. When the box came up, Henrietta felt a thrill of excitement.

"There it is," Ralph whispered loudly. The man couldn't do anything quietly.

"I know," she said in a voice only barely above the sound of the wind. "Try to remain calm."

"Oh. Right."

She waited as they described the box as a hand-carved jewelry box from the early eighties. She wasn't certain that was an accurate date or a correct depiction of what the box was, but by that account, it would run much less on the price spectrum. Or so she hoped.

The bidding began, and she stepped into it with a small bid. A few others showed interested in it but as soon as it neared five hundred dollars, everyone else seemed to lose interest. All the better for her.

She was about to make the winning bid when a hand rose in the back.

"You almost had it," Ralph said.

She shot him a look. She didn't need his distraction at the moment.

Henrietta raised her bid, as did the other bidder. It was hard to see who it was that was bidding. She thought the hand looked small enough to be a woman but, encased in black gloves, it was hard to tell. Even then, it was odd. The temperature did not warrant gloves, that was certain.

Then again, she reasoned, those who came to auctions like these often walked to the beat of their own drum, as her mother would have said.

"How high will you go?" Ralph asked, his voice only slightly lower than the auctioneer.

"Shhhh," she said, leveling a glare at him. He seemed to diminish slightly and allowed her to turn back to the bidding.

She and the other bidder took turns raising the price until Henrietta was almost to the breaking point. She could go further, but *should* she was the question. Then again, the very fact that there was someone else willing to spend well over a thousand dollars on a jewelry box, hand-carved or otherwise, made her curious.

When the gavel finally struck the podium denoting her the winner, Ralph let out a whoop that disturbed most of the room and Henrietta allowed herself a small smile of satisfaction. She'd won, though at a rather exorbitant cost. Not that she couldn't afford it, but still.

She stood abruptly, trying to see who had bid against her. All she saw was the back of a wide brimmed hat leaving the room. Odd.

"Do we go get it now?" Ralph asked, his expression reminding her of a puppy waiting for a new toy.

"We go *pay* and then we 'get it'."

"Hey, as long as you're paying, it doesn't matter to me what we do. Who would have thought these auction thingies would be so exciting?"

She laughed at that and directed him to follow her to the table where she would pay for and retrieve her items. After taking care of it with a swipe from her debit card, she took the wrapped items and left with Ralph trailing behind her.

"Where to now?" he asked when they were back in her Mini Cooper.

"The shop. I want Olivia to start investigating what I've purchased immediately. Forget the to-do list. This is top priority."

"Can I request a stop on the way then?"

"Where?" she asked, gunning the engine and shooting back from their grassy parking space.

Ralph hurried to buckle his seatbelt and gripped the door. "Uh," he said, swallowing loudly, "Frank's Shrimp Shack."

"You're hungry already?"

"It's almost noon."

"Try eleven-thirty."

"I got up early."

She glanced sideways at him and his grin convinced her that a quick stop for popcorn shrimp wasn't completely out of the picture. It was also on the way, she reminded herself, as if she needed to give herself permission to take the time to make the stop.

"Fine. Let's go."

She accelerated quickly when they reached the main road and, before they knew it, she was turning off toward a bright, coral-colored shack near the ocean. She had heard a lot about Frank's from customers to the shop, but she'd never been herself, though she was a bit of an anomaly for those living near the coast in that she didn't often eat seafood.

"You going to get anything?" he asked as they stepped from the car.

"Perhaps," she said, eyeing him. "What will you get?"

"Not sure. Never been here."

"Really?"

"Yes, really." He shrugged and took in the shack. "Marjory didn't really like shrimp."

The cool feeling that coursed through Henrietta had nothing to do with the breeze coming in from the ocean. For all of their teasing and harping on one another, Henrietta and Ralph had an interesting past that, at times like this, came out in painful silence and a feeling of guilt. At least on Henrietta's part.

She had been best friends with Marjory, Ralph's late wife. They had grown up spending time at each other's homes, playing with dolls together, and sharing their secret crushes all the way through middle school When Marjory had moved away with her family, they had become pen pals and stayed in touch that way.

A few summer visits during high school held their friendship together, but they had lost touch as college began. It was only when they both ended up moving back to their home town of Heart's Grove years later that they renewed their friendship. By that time, Marjory was married to Ralph and he'd been a natural addition to the friendship.

Three years had passed since Marjory's death, but Henrietta still felt the slices of guilt at spending time with her best friend's husband. At times, she wondered if he had considered more than friendship with her, but it wasn't something Henrietta wanted to entertain, so she made sure to keep their friendship solidified with lots of sarcasm and emotional distance.

It usually worked.

"I'd forgotten that."

He didn't say anything, merely nodded and held the door open for her.

The scent of shrimp permeated the air as they stepped into the cool interior of the building and were greeted by a friendly young man with braces and brick red hair.

"Hiya, welcome to Frank's. What can I get ya?"

"I'd like to speak with the owner," Frank said, shocking Henrietta. She looked up at him, but he didn't seem to notice, or he chose not to.

"I'll go get him. Hold on."

"What's this all about?" she asked, but any reply was put on hold by the presence of a rotund man wearing a dirty apron and a hairnet.

"I'm Frank. You lookin' for me?" he said with an accent Henrietta couldn't quite place.

"Yes. Name's Ralph Gershwin of Gershwin Private Investigators. This is my partner Henrietta."

She scowled at him before flashing a smile at the man.

"What can I do for ya?"

"We were wondering if we could ask you a few questions. Privately."

"Ah sure," he said, glancing at the young man. "Take the shop for a bit."

Henrietta followed them as they went back outside to sit by a table to the side of the Shack, and she began to wonder just what she'd gotten herself into.

"Look, if this is about that birthday party, I will tell you same as I told that bum Staffordson. I did the number of shrimps they'd paid for—nothing more nothing less." The man threw up his hands as he walked around to a chair and threw himself down on it.

Henrietta was worried the thin, plastic legs might not hold his girth, but they stayed firm even as Frank shook his head violently.

"No, it's nothing like that." Ralph sat down across from the man and Henrietta took the chair next to him.

Henrietta wondered if it wasn't about that, what *was* all of this about?

"I'd like to know what you can tell me about this young woman."

Frank leaned forward, as Henrietta did, both angling for a look at the person in the photograph.

"Oh," Frank said, sitting back and suddenly looking uneasy.

Henrietta frowned at Ralph. She wanted to get his attention and silently ask who in the world the girl was, but then it hit her. She was his missing person.

Realization was quickly followed by frustration. Ralph *had* a lead that he'd disregarded to share with her *and* he'd managed to bring her in on the case without her even realizing it.

"Well?" Ralph asked. Gone was the innocent, friend-to-everyone exterior and in its place, Ralph had taken up his hardened detective exterior. It was more intense than intimidating, but it sufficed to bring Frank up in his seat.

"Okay, so I helped the girl. And I may have paid her under the table a little bit, but she's gone now. I swear."

"I'm just a P.I.," Ralph reminded him. "I'm not attached to the law at this point and neither is this case, so you're in no trouble. What can you tell me about her?"

"Well…" Frank rubbed his jaw. "Said her name was Christen and that she was trying to get away from a bad relationship. Abuse or some such thing. I'm *not* okay with that. Always taught my boys you treat a lady like you would your own mother—or better," he added with raised eyebrows.

Ralph nodded, encouraging him on.

"I never had girls of my own, but I'm a big softie, just ask anyone." Frank shrugged. "I told her she could bus some tables and make a little under the table. Just enough to get her where she was going, you know?"

"Do you know where she was staying while she worked here?"

"Not really. I think she took the bus somewhere."

"You remember what bus?"

"Nah." Frank shook his head. Then, a light came into his eyes. "Oh yeah! I did see her one day. She got on the Eastbound. Number...thirty-three, I think it was. Don't know where she was heading, though."

"That's great," Ralph said encouragingly.

"Did she say where she was going?"

"How much did she make?"

Henrietta and Ralph's questions fell on top of one another, and Frank looked between them. Quite the pair of detectives, Henrietta thought.

"Did she say where she was heading after here?" Ralph asked, shooting Henrietta a look. She wanted to remind him that he had brought her along on this, but she would tell him that at a later time.

"Nope. I'm not sure she really knew herself. She seemed..." Frank rubbed his chin. "Lost."

Ralph nodded, and Henrietta took the chance to speak up again. "How much, approximately, would you say that she earned while working here?"

"Not much," Frank said, shrugging. "Maybe five hundred and some change. Well, I did give her a couple extra hundred on her last day. Felt bad for her and all."

"You're a good man," Ralph said with a kind smile

toward the man. "If I think of any more questions, I'll stop by."

"Sure thing. You guys want some shrimp?" Ralph grinned and that was all the encouragement the man needed. "Stay here. A Shrimp Shack special for you both coming up."

When he was gone, Ralph turned to her. "What's this about not wanting to be involved?"

She knew he meant the question she'd asked, but she wasn't going to let him get away that easily.

"*You* were the one that brought me here under false pretense."

"False pre— You've got to be kidding me." He rolled his eyes in an exaggerated manner. "What's so bad about a working lunch?"

"It's your working lunch, not mine."

"And yet you asked a question. Why? Why do you care how much she made?"

"I just… I don't know. I'm curious, I suppose."

"Thinking of changing careers?" he asked with a grin.

"Hardly."

They enjoyed a delicious shrimp meal compliments of Frank and then set off for town again. The whole while, Henrietta contemplated the photo of the young woman. She had large, vacant blue eyes and a round face framed by long, stringy black hair. Her expression reminded Henrietta of a magazine model who was told to 'look disinterested' in everything. She captured the look well.

"What else have you not told me you know about this young woman?" she asked.

"Why the sudden interest?"

Despite the lack of emotion in the girl's face, something about her screamed for help. Henrietta had never been able to turn down someone in need.

"What else?"

"She went dormant on all social media shortly after her disappearance. One post showed an image of downtown New York with a cryptic caption about how short life is. Scott felt like it could have been to throw people off her trail, make them think she'd committed suicide, but I don't think so."

"What do you think?" she asked as they turned onto the main thoroughfare of their quaint town.

"I honestly don't know," he said.

She glanced at him, but he sat there, cramped with his knees bent, staring ahead. "Anything else?" she asked in a soft voice.

"Not really. We've got the name and contact info of her best friend, but she hasn't returned any of my calls."

"Have you texted her?"

"Huh?"

Henrietta shrugged. "I've just noticed that when I call the youth of my church to ask about helping at the shop or what have you, they never respond, but if I text them, I almost always get an immediate reply."

"I hadn't thought to text her. Seemed a bit impersonal."

"To be sure," Henrietta said, pulling up to her parking spot in the back of H.H. Antiques. "But she can't blame you for trying."

"Good idea. I'll do that. And, Henri…" He brandished a teasing grin at her. "Good to have you on the case."

"Henrietta!" Olivia's excited shout caught Henrietta in the middle of dusting one of their display cases. She jolted up and nearly rammed her head on one of the glass shelves.

Taking a deep, steadying breath, she calmly put down her feather duster and headed for the front room. She found her assistant sitting behind the computer, nose inches from the screen. That couldn't be healthy.

"What is it?"

"You are not going to believe this."

"Well?" she asked, not wanting to wait any longer for the apparently big news.

"It's worth almost ten times what you paid for it." Olivia still hadn't taken her gaze from the screen and was furiously clicking back and forth.

"Why don't you start by telling me what antique we're talking about?"

"Oh, sorry." Olivia finally looked away from the captivating screen and pushed her glasses up. "The puzzle box."

"The what?"

"Your auction box." She indicated the box on the other side of the computer. "It's a Japanese-style puzzle box circa 1960 made by a famous wood carver, Salvatore Green. He was rumored to have toured this area and I think this is one of perhaps five boxes of his left *in the world*."

"Oh my," Henrietta said, pulling a chair over to the small table. "Tell me more."

"Well, I started with the style and got nowhere, so I began searching the initials inside the box."

"Initials?"

"Yes. S. G. I mean, it wasn't much to go on and I wasn't hoping for much, but when I added in wood carving and box, something like what you have popped up. The rest is history," she said with a girlish giggle.

"But you said puzzle box. This doesn't resemble any puzzle box I've seen."

"That threw me off a little as well. Apparently, he created Japanese-style puzzle boxes that looked like regular jewelry boxes but contained secret compartments. It's ingenious really. Create something that looks like something else but isn't."

"Is there a way to open it?" Henrietta asked.

"Not that I've seen. I found a few of his other boxes on line. One had a YouTube tutorial, but I tried—very gently—to open it like they showed and no such luck. I found one blogger who said he liked to make each puzzle box differently so that no one box could open like the other. Figures." She shook her head and looked at the box. "What secrets are you hiding?" she asked it.

"I wish we knew," Henrietta added.

"I'll keep looking, though. There are a ton more forums on this guy's artwork and on puzzle boxes in general. I'm sure I can find some tips and tricks or something. A 'How to open an antique puzzle box for dummies' would be great right about now."

Henrietta smiled and nodded. "Good to know. In the meantime, when you're not *very carefully* attempting to open the box, let's keep it in the safe. Just in case."

"Absolutely." Olivia turned to her employer. "Are you still going to offer it up as the silent auction item this year? There's no way anyone would be able to bid what it's worth."

"Considering I made a killing on it, I think it may still do just that. But we shall see."

Olivia seemed to take her answer in stride and turned back to the screen for more research.

"Make sure you don't stay too late," Henrietta cautioned, knowing her employee's penchant for working past her clock-out time.

"Nelson's working late tonight. I might as well do something productive." She shrugged and grinned up at Henrietta.

"Just as long as you're sure."

"Absolutely. I'm hooked on this mystery."

Henrietta nodded and made her way back to the case she was cleaning. She was hooked as well, but for a different reason. Was it possible that her opposing bidder knew the true worth of the puzzle box? Was that the cause for the challenge?

Scrunching up her nose, she reached for her phone and brought up the number of the estate auction supervisor.

"Hello, Coast Estates Auction House. This is Millicent Bedford speaking."

"Hello, Millicent, this is Henrietta Hewitt of H.H. Antiques."

"Ah, Miss Hewitt, good to hear from you. I do hope this is not about any dissatisfaction of your purchases from our recent auction."

"No, nothing like that. I actually had a question regarding the auction."

"Yes?"

Henrietta could picture Millicent. She was four years older and was a senior when Henrietta had gone into high school. Her light blonde hair had always been perfectly styled, and Henrietta was sure the same was true to this day.

"I was curious if you had any extra information on the man whose estate was auctioned off."

"Did you get the info packet we sent in the mail?"

"Yes." She thought back to the generic biography that had been included. "It was...lacking."

"Well..." Henrietta could tell that it had been Millicent herself who had composed the packet. "I suppose there was more to the man than what was included, but we don't have limitless funds with which to create materials and—"

"I just want to know a little bit more about the house and the artifacts included in the auction. I'm sure it was too much information to send out in one small, well-written packet." She shamelessly added the compliment hoping that the woman didn't see it for what it was: pure bribery.

"Oh, I'm pleased to know you thought that. I actually did compile quite a bit of research on Mister Patton. Would you like me to email it over?"

"If you could, that would be wonderful."

"From one history lover to another, his backstory leaves quite the impression."

"I'm sure."

"Ta-ta," Millicent said before the line went dead.

Knowing Millicent—or, more likely, her reputation —as Henrietta did, she had assumed this would be the case. The woman was thorough with a capital T.

Only a few moments later, her phone buzzed, and she swiped it open to see the email from Millicent. As she navigated to her email, her finger paused over an unrecognized sender. The subject line was left blank, something that almost always made her click delete, but something about the email address made her tap it open.

Printed in a strange font, the only text in the whole email was one line:

Do not sell the puzzle box—or else!

4

"If you think that one threatening email, if you can even call it that, is going to keep me from putting the puzzle box up for the silent auction, you have completely lost your skills as a detective."

Ralph sat across from Henrietta at her kitchen table, Sepia prowling around their feet in search of dropped bits of the turkey sandwich Ralph had brought from the deli on the corner.

"I don't think that, but it is my suggestion."

"And when have you ever known me to turn tail and run when things get tough?"

"Never, but—"

"And who really thought that email would intimidate me? 'Or else.' What is that even supposed to mean? Or else they'll throw eggs at my shop? Or else they'll stick their tongue out at me? There are a lot of options here."

Ralph couldn't help but grin at her tirade, something that made her even more incensed. "I'm serious, Ralph. What did they hope to accomplish?"

"Fear?"

She stopped pacing the small kitchen and stared him down, hands on hips. "Fear? From that terribly written, poorly communicated note? I mean, who threatens anyone with email?"

"It is the twenty-first century, you know."

"That's neither here nor there."

"What are you going to do?"

"Do?" Now she threw her hands into the air in an act of exasperation. "Am I supposed to email them back and say 'okie-dokie'? As if I'd cave that easily."

"I repeat, what are you going to do?"

"I have no idea."

"Want me to have Scott look into it?"

"Not yet. But maybe soon."

"Henri, what are you thinking?" Ralph's eyes narrowed.

"Honestly?" She slid into the chair opposite him. "I'm thinking that I need to figure out all I can about this puzzle box. And fast."

"How can I help?"

His response surprised her. While they had collaborated on a few of his cases in the past, she'd never come to him with help. Then again, she'd never needed to. The question was, did the sender of the email have evil intentions, or were they perhaps the embittered bidder who hadn't gotten what they wanted and resorted to sending threatening emails instead?

"I'm honestly not sure."

He leaned back, his chair squeaking loudly and sending Sepia running off toward the living room. Henrietta stared into nothingness, contemplating her next move. She was spitting mad that someone had dared to threaten her, but she was also intrigued.

"Perhaps you can ask around about Mister Gerald Patton for me."

"And he is?"

"*Was* the man whose house we visited."

"Ah, rich, older man. Got it."

"A deceased, rich, older man, so please use tact."

"When am I not tactful?"

She opened her mouth to reply but saw that Ralph's eyes were twinkling.

"Why am I here?" he said after she failed to respond.

"Oh, yes, I need your assistance with weapons."

His eyebrows rose. "Pardon me?"

"There's a gun dating back to the Civil War and I need you to make sure it's functional but also disarmed."

His grin widened. She knew he worked with Civil War reenactments and spent countless hours with old firearms, in addition to new ones. Locally, and even statewide, he was known as something of an expert. She could tell he was enjoying the fact that she'd called on his expertise for once.

"Lead the way, madam," he said, making an overexaggerated bow.

She chose not to respond and headed back downstairs, Sepia trailing close behind. There was a cat door that allowed her full access to the whole house, but she often stayed where the action was. A girl after Henrietta's own heart.

"Say, Henri," Ralph said, his voice distant behind her on the narrow back hallway that led to the office space on the main floor.

"How many times do I have to tell you *not* to call me that?'

"At least a few more." His smile was white teeth against darkness until she turned on the light, nearly blinding them both. "You'd think that a scared young woman trying to hide would leave a place where she was spotted, wouldn't you?'

"Yes. Of course. Why do you ask?" She knew he was talking about Cybil, but she wanted to hear his full explanation.

"Cybil's photo has been splashed all over news outlets—her parents' doing. They are using social media to its fullest advantage posing as concerned parents who just want to find their daughter."

Henrietta stopped, spinning on her heel. "Posing?"

Ralph grimaced. "I'm sure they care about her…"

"But?"

"I don't know." He rubbed the back of his neck. "It seems a bit much. I read her note and it sounded as if she was of sound mind and making a decision to try it on her own. What they're doing is…over the top."

"You don't agree with their tactics?"

"I don't agree with their motives."

"Which are?"

"I don't know."

Henrietta studied Ralph. He wasn't one given to strictly following his gut instinct unless there was evidence to back it up, but in this case, he seemed to be solely working on instinct.

"Perhaps it takes being in that situation to understand their perspective."

"If Scott went off on his own but left a note like she had… I don't know." He rubbed his neck again then followed her into the sitting room, where she had locked glass cases with firearms on display. "I would be concerned but I don't think I'd go to their lengths. I'd have to trust that what he'd decided to do was best for him."

Henrietta pulled out the pistol and a length of velvet fabric, laying it over the top of a glass case nearby before she turned to him. "But you took their case."

"That was when I thought there was one."

"You don't think Cybil is lost."

"I don't know what to think of Cybil Markham, but I have a feeling she's the furthest thing from lost. Her actions say…calculated."

That took Henrietta by surprise. "What are you going to do?"

He grinned. "Seems like I was asking you that just a few minutes ago."

"Two peas in a pod," she said, shrugging.

"Yep." He held her gaze for a little too long and she looked away and back to the gun between them. "I suppose we can both wait it out and see what happens. Together."

"I suppose."

The silence stretched between them, filled only with the sounds of metal parts clinking. Henrietta wasn't sure what was more dangerous: a threatening email or being in accord with Ralph.

Henrietta needed coffee more than ever. She'd tossed and turned, her mind alternating between replaying her conversation with Ralph and scrolling the threatening email in front of her mind's eye. It wasn't so much a threat in the daylight, but last night, it had loomed more after Ralph's caution. He, of course, was merely concerned with her well-being, but that made her jumpy.

"Hen-ri-et-ta." Gina sashayed out from behind the counter in *Espresso Yourself* with her arms outstretched. Her dyed, spiky black hair had pink tips and she wore so much jewelry she sounded like Ebenezer Scrooge's chained ghost. "You look like you need about ten extra shots of espresso. Don't worry, doll. We'll get you fixed right up. But come here first."

Henrietta found herself being pulled into the perfume-scented embrace of her next-door neighbor, fellow business owner, and good friend, Gina Russo. Her Italian heritage to blame, or so she claimed, Gina had never met a stranger in her life and would offer you coffee or food no matter the time of day, believing that it fixed most things.

"Are you ready for the festival? Only a few days before the proverbial flood gates are opened. I've been roasting coffee like my life depended on it." She shook her head, the large, chunky earrings she wore swinging back and forth.

"I think we're just about there. I got a little distracted." Henrietta thought of the puzzle box sitting in her safe. Should she seriously consider pulling it from the silent auction? Then again, how had someone even known she was going to auction it off? She hadn't told anyone what her submission would be, not even Mayor Ricky. Interesting.

"What do you have scampering around up there?" Gina asked, twirling her index finger in the air. "I see…something."

While Henrietta loved her friend, she also knew that the surest way to spread any news through the whole town was to tell Gina Russo.

"Nothing. Just thinking about what's still on my list."

"Oh, honey, it'll get done. And what doesn't wasn't really that important to begin with."

Henrietta could argue that, thinking that she didn't put anything on a list that wasn't crucial, but there was no convincing Gina of something she held as a truism.

"What do you have on special today for baked goods. I need coffee and some sort of pastry if I'm going to make it through the morning."

"Oh, do we have a treat for you," Gina said, dodging a few customers as she walked around the counter. "These new lemon lavender scones are the absolute best thing you'll ever taste. Scout's honor."

"I somehow don't think you were ever a scout," Henrietta observed, "but I'll take one nonetheless."

Gina let out a cackle of a laugh and reached into the glass case to retrieve a scone. "You've got it. And the usual for your drink?"

"Yes, please."

"Coming right up."

Henrietta took a seat at one of the empty tables, eyeing the scone that Gina had slid into a small paper bag. It looked good and she was sure it would taste even better. Gina's baker came in early every morning to bake. Sometimes Henrietta thought it would be the best job. Up early, baking in the quiet, and then going home. But then considering the fact she'd have to be up by four every morning, the reality was less enticing than it sounded.

"Here you are," Gina said, coming around the counter with a to-go cup containing Henrietta's non-fat vanilla latte. "I put in an extra shot. I'm sure you'll thank me later."

"I'll thank you now," she said with a laugh.

Henrietta left the shop, the scent of coffee dissipating slightly in the open air. That was one great thing about being next to a coffee shop. You always had the slight scent of coffee to surround you.

She stopped in front of her shop and envisioned the setup she would have for the festival. The front yard of H.H. Antiques was well maintained, the grass green and trimmed neatly thanks to her lawn maintenance man Donny. The flowers that edged the white picket fence shot up in a colorful array and added to the homey sense. She had debated what they would do to bring a little bit of the indoors *outdoors* and had decided on renting a large, white tent for the front yard. It would span across both sides of the lawn, leaving the pathway covered.

Then, with the help of Ralph, Scott, and any other hands she could rope into service, they would bring out many of her larger antique items for display. She also wanted to use a few antique church pews and chairs to create an old-fashioned sitting area. Lastly, per Olivia's suggestion, they were going to pull out some of the items to create a type of photo booth at the back.

The idea was to utilize social media and hashtags—however that worked. Henrietta still wasn't completely sure, but she was letting Olivia run with that part. If it gained her business, she was happy to do it.

"You look like someone who is surveying their kingdom."

Henrietta turned to see Scott, Ralph's son and co-investigator, standing with his hands on his hips.

"I'm mentally preparing for all of the work we're going to do once the tent is up."

He grinned. "Dad told me I was being roped into service. Anything to help you, Henrietta."

"You are rather wonderful," she said, patting his cheek in a motherly way. She'd known Scott since he was born and felt a sense of maternal pride over the boy.

"Morning," a singsong voice said. They both turned to see Olivia ride up on her bike. She hopped off, her t-strap sandals clacking on the pavement.

"H-hi, Olivia," Scott said.

Henrietta didn't miss the way that Scott's neck reddened at the sight of the young woman. It was a shame she was already dating someone.

"What are you both doing out here?" she said, looking between them then up at the large, three-story Victorian that housed H.H. Antiques as well as Henrietta's living quarters.

"Plotting," Henrietta said.

Olivia's eyes widened. "A...book?"

"No, silly girl," she said, not missing the way that Olivia and Scott shared a look. "The plans for the Blackberry Festival."

"Oh, I see." Olivia peered around them. "I think it'll turn out really well. Sure to entice people in to the yard and then hopefully on to the house. I'm excited for the photo booth."

Scott took interest in this, to no surprise of Henrietta's, and he and Olivia began to talk social media and hashtags and following and Henrietta lost complete interest. Thankfully, Ralph showed up not long after.

"Was wondering when you'd show up," she said, taking a sip of her coffee and wishing she'd already succumbed to the enticing, sweet but tangy scent of the scone.

"How'd you know I would?"

"Usually, when Scott comes to the shop, you're not far behind." She gave in and pulled off a corner of the pastry. The tart frosting mingled with the lavender and lemon flavors perfectly, making her close her eyes momentarily. Perfection.

"Care to share?" he said with a grin.

"No. You can get your own." She savored another bite then met his gaze. "You have something new about the case, don't you?"

His eyebrows rose, but he knew better than to be too surprised.

"I do. Care for a trip to Sequim?"

Henrietta sighed heavily. There was so much to do to get the shop ready for the festival, but, while she'd be loath to admit it, she had a vested interest in this case now.

"That's a yes, isn't it?" he said, leaning toward her with a grin. She hadn't said anything, but he knew her well enough to read her expressions.

"Scott, we'll be back. You two hold down the fort."

Scott looked at once shocked and thrilled, while Olivia looked to Scott then back to Henrietta.

"We need to run an errand down to Sequim. I'll be back by lunchtime for your break."

"No problem," Olivia said, sending another furtive glance at Scott then back to her. "We'll be fine."

"We-we will," Scott said, as if surprised and agreeing at the same time.

"Henri," Ralph said, grinning down at her, "let's hit the road."

5

Ralph drove a gas-guzzling, Ford F150 that roared to life with the first turn of the key and jerked backward as he pulled out of the graveled lot. She half-expected him to spin in the gravel, but he was a more careful driver than she was. Though she'd never admit that to him.

"Are you going to tell me what we'll be doing? Or do I have to *detect* that?"

"Do you think you could?" he asked, grinning over at her as he pulled onto the highway.

"Let's see," she said, pushing back into the seat to make herself more comfortable.

They were going to Sequim, a slightly larger town than Heart's Grove. He really hadn't said much, but she could guess it had to do with a sighting of the girl—or perhaps someone that had talked with her?

Then she thought of Frank's comment about the

bus Cybil had taken. It was possible she took that to a station in town and then switched to the Sequim bus. If Ralph had been to the bus station earlier that day then he would have been able to confirm that, possibly even with video surveillance. Many in town had known him as a detective with the PD so they would have had no problem cooperating.

She glanced around and caught sight of a coffee cup in the holder near the steering wheel. That was all the confirmation she needed.

"I assume we're going to see where Cybil was staying."

His jaw dropped, and she tried not to enjoy his surprise. At least not too much.

"How...how in tarnation did you divine that?"

"No divination involved. Pure deduction."

"Please, enlighten me."

She sighed, giving in to the desire to grandstand just a little. "Well, first off, I knew it had to be something dealing with Cybil's past—or even current—whereabouts. That's what all this is about anyway, so it's logical."

"Right. Go on."

"So I assumed you followed up on the bus lead, something which your cup of coffee confirmed to me."

"My...my coffee?"

"Yes. It's from that little drive-through shop on the way from your house to the bus station. You always stop there, but only if you're going that way. It 'only makes sense' then, as you often say."

He shrugged, knowing that he did say that.

"So then I assumed you got confirmation that she switched buses at the terminal and found she went to Sequim. It would only make sense to go there if you were staying. She could have been meeting someone as well, but to do so on a regular basis—as I assume she did—likely meant she was staying there. And why not, since it's slightly larger than Heart's Grove and would be a bit easier to hide in."

"Color me impressed," Ralph said. "Just one thing. How did you know that this coffee wasn't from yesterday or a week ago?"

"The coffee stain on your shirt."

He looked down. "Well, shoot." Shaking his head, he looked back at the road. "Henri, you *sure* you don't want a job?"

"Positive. I already have one. Actually, two in reality."

"Don't you go counting writing."

"I don't understand everyone's aversion to my book."

Ralph barely contained a laugh. "Let me put it as gently as I can."

She waited, watching him try to contain his laughter.

"Don't give up your day job."

She rolled her eyes. "You know Hemingway

received over one hundred rejections. I'm sure his friends berated him as well. I shall not give up." She tipped her chin in the air.

"You do that, Henri. You do that." He took the exit for Sequim and they took a winding road to the south end of town.

"While you guessed it, I'll fill you in a little on the specifics."

"Please do." She watched the road, taking in the scenery as he started in on the explanation.

"I did as you say and checked out the bus station. The older ladies behind the counter love me." He wagged his eyebrows, but Henrietta pretended not to notice. "Anyway, they were able to pull the approximate time Cybil would have been there."

"Did you get that from Frank?"

"Yep, stopped by on my way and got some more shrimp."

She almost commented on his newfound love of the shellfish but decided against it. Too many memories.

"We scoured through some minutes of footage until we saw her. Small little waif of a thing. She got on the bus out of town toward Sequim."

"I see. Was the particular bus visible?"

"Yep. Which is how I narrowed it down. I think the motel I found is the most likely one. Plus, the guy at the front desk admitted to seeing someone based on her description, though he wouldn't confirm or deny anything else."

"So do you hope to pester him into it then?" she asked, turning toward him as they pulled off the main road into the small parking lot of a Budget Motel. It looked seedy with a few cars, some of them Henrietta wasn't sure would even run, parked like broken teeth in a fighter's smile.

"No," Ralph said, drawing out the word, "but I do hope to speak with the owner and…reason with him."

She scowled. "What does that mean?"

"To use all my persuasion, and maybe a little bit of yours, to convince him that this is in the girl's best interest."

"That goes against hotel policy!"

"Um hum," he said noncommittally as he pulled into a parking space. "Let's go."

Henrietta followed him, though she couldn't help but scowl. Nothing good, or honest, could come from this.

They stepped into the motel's lobby. Paint that used to be white but had turned a grayish color graced the walls of the small room. A broken vending machine sat in one corner with two chairs on either side. A TV with a cracked screen played the local news, and a man with hair the color of the walls sat behind a desk.

He looked up when they came in, then looked back down.

"Charming," she whispered and got an elbow jabbed gently in her side.

"Good morning," Ralph said with more cheer than the location deserved.

"Yeah, be with ya in a second."

Henrietta was relatively certain the man wasn't busy, merely taking his sweet time.

When he finally turned to them, his eyes went from Ralph to Henrietta then back to Ralph. "You two want a room?"

"Certainly not," Henrietta said.

Ralph shot her another look and leaned against the counter. "Actually, we came for some information. We're private investigators."

Henrietta was sure that there was some type of law against lumping her in with Ralph's agency, but she decided to remain silent about it just this once. Instead, she took in the man's body language to this news. His shoulders tensed, and he immediately looked anxious. Anxious reactions usually indicated a person was hiding something. What was this man's secret?

"I ain't got to answer no questions from anyone who's not the police."

Her gaze roamed the desk behind the man. "True," she said, taking another step forward, "but if you'd prefer us not to mention your tax fraud to the local authorities, perhaps you could answer our very innocuous questions and we'd be on our way."

"M-my tax... Just what do you two want?"

Ralph's smile broadened. "This girl." He pulled out a

photo of Cybil. "I have reason to believe she is—or was —staying at this location. Can you confirm that?"

The man looked conflicted, odd to Henrietta considering his willingness to commit other crimes. "We can assure you we're acting in her best interests. Her parents are looking for her."

"She claimed she was eighteen, old enough to get her own room without questions from the likes of me."

"And as long as she paid in cash, I'm sure you were *very* happy."

He scowled. "Look, she was nice and looked scared. We get all types here, and I'm not one to question. I'm nobody's guardian."

"How charming," Henrietta commented. Ralph scowled at her and looked back at the man.

"She's not, by chance, still checked in here, is she?"

"Nah, you just missed her. 'Er, if she was here. You know." He tried to look penitent for giving away the information, but it didn't work. "Checked out a day or so ago. Can't remember."

"May we see the room she was in?"

"What? You think we don't have cleaners? It's already been done."

"Mmm." Ralph nodded thoughtfully. "May we see it anyway?"

"You know what?" The man leaned down beneath the counter and pulled out an old-fashioned key attached to a diamond-shaped fob. "Knock yourselves out. Number ten."

"Thanks. We'll get this back to you."

The man waved his hand but shot a look at Henrietta as if to make sure she really was going to hold up her end of the bargain and not turn him in. She merely stared back until he looked away again.

"After you," Ralph said through gritted teeth.

"Thank you."

They walked toward number ten and Ralph let out a sigh. "When I said persuasion, I didn't mean blackmail. And how did you know he's committing tax fraud?"

"You didn't specify, and I thought suggesting he help us was in all our best interests. And I thought he was doing a crossword but when we approached the counter, I realized it wasn't that at all. It looks like he's keeping two sets of books. One no doubt tallying what he gets in cash and the other what he reports."

"You're too much," Ralph said, but she noted his smile.

They approached the door and he fitted the key to the lock. The door groaned on un-oiled hinges and swung open to reveal a sparse room. A bed, dresser with lopsided TV that looked like it was from the early 90s, and a nightstand with a lamp took up most of the room. The bathroom, with fixtures that also looked like they were from twenty years ago, peeked through a narrow doorway at the back of the room.

"Charming," she said again.

"Let's see what Miss Cybil left behind," Ralph said.

They took half an hour searching through the room but to no avail. As they were just about ready to give up, a shadow darkened the doorway. Henrietta looked up from where she had been looking under the bed, and Ralph stood up so quickly he nearly knocked the bedside lamp off.

"I thought of something that might help you all out." It was the man from the front desk. His bushy hair was wind-tossed from his walk to the room, but he looked in better spirits than he had before.

"What's that?" Ralph said, obvious enthusiasm in his voice.

"You said her parents were looking for her and all that, and I just got thinking that if my boy went missing, I'd want to know where he was."

"Right," Ralph said, trying to urge the man on past the emotional ties.

"Anyway." He reached out and roughed a hand over the day's growth on his chin. "When she checked out, she said something about a 'more permanent' arrangement. I assume living. And that she'd no longer have to take the bus. I didn't know where she was going, but I'd see her out there at the stop most days. I figured, good for her—getting on her feet and all. So, there's that."

"Thank you," Ralph said, stepping forward to shake

the man's hand. "And here's the key. We've seen all we needed to."

"Yeah, well, you're welcome," the man said, accepting the key.

They left, and Henrietta wondered just what type of permanent residence a young woman could find after leaving a job.

They climbed into Ralph's truck and headed back toward Heart's Grove. "So she just left. Seems...odd," Ralph commented.

"And for something more permanent. But she also left her job at Frank's."

"Right." Ralph took a hand from the steering wheel and rubbed at his jaw. "It's not adding up."

"Do you think she's still around here? What's to say she didn't leave the area?"

"That's a good question. I'm not sure."

"And why is she here in the first place?"

"Another good question."

Henrietta stared out the window, eyes narrowed. "It would seem like this young woman came here for a reason. It's *very* specific to come to Heart's Grove. Almost polar opposite of New York—as the United States goes."

"I agree. I tried to get that information from her family, but they seem insistent that they have no idea. That she left, and her last credit card purchase was a ticket here. I almost would have told them it was a ruse if we hadn't found evidence that she was, in fact, here."

"So there has to be a reason." Henrietta began bobbing her head up and down. "She wouldn't have come here without one."

"Boyfriend maybe?

"Then why stay in that motel?"

"We can rule out job if she was willing to work at Frank's under the table for a time."

"And we can also rule out a random choice."

"What makes you say that?"

"Because she's stayed around. She was so committed to being here, she got a cheap hotel in a larger area and bussed her way to a job that would pay her under the table for a time. Almost as if..." Henrietta's mind whirled.

"What?" Ralph glanced at her. "I know that look. What are you thinking?"

"It's almost as if she *wanted* to be at Frank's."

"The man's son?"

"Not likely if she left the job." Henrietta thought of the area. "I'm not sure. It just seems very...specific."

They took the exit for Heart's Grove and Ralph turned down the main street to drop Henrietta off at the shop. When he pulled up out front, he put the truck in park and turned to her. "You think that she *wanted* to be near Frank's?"

"Yes, but I have no idea why."

He nodded his head, eyes narrowed and staring into the distance. "Then that's what we've got to find out."

6

A shrill blaring sound woke Henrietta from a dead sleep. She sat up in bed, clutching at her pounding heart and trying to make sense of what was going on.

The alarm. Her alarm was going off.

She jumped from bed, nearly tripping on Sepia, her tail the size of a feather duster in her shock at being awoken in such a rude manner.

"Goodness," Henrietta said to herself. In all the years she'd had the shop, the alarm had only gone off one other time and it had been due to a pesky squirrel who got a little too zealous with a wire. She hoped that was the case now.

She wrapped herself in a lightweight robe and stepped into a pair of flip flops, hesitating at the doorway to the hall from her bedroom. She knew that her alarm company would have already alerted the police and would no doubt be calling her to confirm it was, in fact, an emergency, but she felt sudden hesitation about going downstairs.

When she'd first moved into the top two stories of the large Victorian home, she'd installed a door between the levels. It rested at the top of a long, narrow staircase that led to the first floor. It was always locked at the end of the day when she retired upstairs. At the time, it had seemed like a silly, and slightly costly, addition, but now she was glad for it.

Now, standing at the door, she hesitated. She was transported back to the first year after she'd moved in. The transition from living with a roommate to living alone had been something of a brutal experience. She'd almost adjusted but every night as she'd close the door, she felt she was closing herself off just a little.

Years of living on her own save for Sepia had taught her to enjoy the silent moments and to make sure she got out of the house frequently. So far, it had seemed to work.

Tonight, however, she wished she didn't live alone.

As if reminding her both of their lives were at stake, Sepia rubbed up against her legs, her tail returned to its normal size.

"Oh fine, I'll be the brave one and check on things for the both of us," she said to the cat.

She unlocked the door and started down the steps. The alarm was even louder in the stairwell and she fought the urge to cover her ears. At the bottom of the stairs, she looked around, uncertain of what she'd find.

The phone was ringing, as she'd expected, and she supposed that should be the first place she went. To the counter and the phone.

Eerie red lights flashed on and off at the location of the alarm siren and she used its strobe effect to make her way through the darkness to the desk. When she picked up the phone, she had to plug her other ear to hear the woman on the other end of the line.

She told the lady from the alarm company she had no idea what was going on and that it was best for the police to come, and then was reassured by the woman they had already been dispatched and would be arriving soon.

The woman cautioned her to stay on the line, but she assured her that she needed to be there when the police arrived at the front of the building because there was no way she would allow them to break the antique glass in her front door to gain entrance. She hung up despite the woman's protests.

She picked her way through the narrow aisle toward the front door and suddenly felt a swirl of wind. Pausing, her heart pounding in her ears despite the ringing of the alarm, she swallowed and looked around.

Nothing seemed to be out of place except for the breeze. Why was there a breeze?

When she stepped around the corner, she came to a stop, mouth dropping open. No wonder the alarm had gone off—the front door was wide open to the night, allowing the sounds of the alarm to permeate to darkness.

She stepped closer, her eyes wide and ready to flee at the first sign of any movement, but nothing changed. The alarm still blared. The door still stood open. Then she heard the sirens. Heart's Grove wasn't large, so she was surprised it had taken the police so long to get there. Then again, perhaps time had felt slower than it was.

Reaching the door, she slowed and saw something folded beneath the open door. It looked as if it had been trapped by the door but when she bent to retrieve it, she saw that it looked as if it had been purposefully placed there.

Gripping only the edge of the note, she picked it up from the top and let it flutter open. Knowing the police were coming, she flipped on the front porch light and stepped out. The note was simple enough:

I warned you. Take your auction item down, or next time I won't be so harmless.

A chill raced up her spine at the words. While they weren't exactly the most ominous words she'd read, they did disturb her. Someone knew that she was auctioning off the puzzle box for the festival and was determined to get her to change her mind.

Looking back at the open door, she saw it for what it was. A warning. But what a foolish one. They had somehow managed to pick her lock, not a difficult feat she was sure, but they had to have known about the alarm. There was a plaque in the front flower garden that stated just that. So it had been purposeful.

She looked around uneasily. The street looked much the same as it did in the daytime, though now shrouded in darkness. Was it possible someone was out there watching her?

The coming police lights shot red and blue around like a paint-gun and she began to breathe easier. She would let them search the shop and house portions just to be sure and hand them the letter to see if they could find anything. It was doubtful, since most criminals, no matter how inexperienced, knew enough to wear gloves usually.

"Ma'am?" a younger officer said, climbing from his squad car. "Are you all right?"

Was she?

Henrietta hardly knew what to say to that. She was physically all right, but mentally, she was shaken. That was likely the exact response the person who had left the note wanted. To rattle her and make her change her mind about the puzzle box. Well, she wasn't going to give them the satisfaction. Henrietta Hewitt didn't back down due to intimidation or fearmongering.

"I am all right. I'd like you to look inside, though."

Her safe flashed to mind. She should have checked to make sure the box was even there!

"You betcha. We're coming in."

She felt the tension in her chest release slightly. She wasn't alone. They would figure this out. It would be all right.

"Why didn't you call me?" Ralph stood before her, his hands on his hips with a stare leveled at her.

"The police were here. What else could you have done?"

"I don't know." He tossed his hands in the air and began to pace in front of her at the center of the shop where she was dusting, yet again. "Stayed here after they left."

"You were going to camp out on my antique sofa? That's very kind of you, but I reset the alarm—which did its job, by the way—and went to bed. End of story." Well, that was mostly the end of the story. She had laid awake in bed for at least two hours after the incident and had flinched at every sound, but she *had* finally gone to sleep.

"Henri." He stopped pacing and stared at her. "I worry about you here all alone."

"I'm not alone." She turned back to her dusting. "I have Sepia."

"Oh yeah, how could I forget your very special feline companion."

"She provides sufficient company." When he didn't respond, she snuck a glance at him to find his gaze on her, assessing.

She put down her dust cloth and faced him, but what could she say? Yes, she had thought about calling him, but she hadn't. Why? Because he was her best friend's husband and shouldn't be the first person she thought of in a crisis. Or, most of the time.

"Henri, I care about you. I care about your safety. I want to be here...for you."

Oh no. No, no. He couldn't look at her like that with those soft eyes and the expression that conveyed much more than she was willing to accept.

"Thank you, but I was fine. We were fine," she amended, seeing Sepia in her usual perch atop the grandfather clock.

He arched an eyebrow but didn't say anything.

Olivia burst into the room with a bright expression. "I think I found something out about our box!"

Henrietta looked from Olivia to Ralph then back to Olivia. "Do enlighten us."

"Follow me," she said, motioning them to follow her to the backroom where the safe was kept and where she had been observing the box in an attempt to find out more about its origins.

"I don't get it," Ralph said, squeezing into the small

room with the women. "Don't you already know about this thing?"

"Yes and no," Olivia answered. "It came with a vague descriptive paper, but that was almost no help and most of the information on it was wrong. I don't understand it. When something like that goes to auction, it's supposed to be appraised…but I digress."

"Well, don't keep us in suspense," Henrietta prompted.

"Oh yes." Olivia walked to the other side of the large table and put both fingers on the box. Suddenly, a small drawer popped out.

"Wha—what just happened?" Ralph said.

"That's not all," Olivia said. She gently pressed down on the piece that had popped out and a thin sliver of wood slid from the bottom. Taking great care, she turned it over and showed the inner workings of the box.

"Is that a combination lock?"

"It is," Olivia agreed.

"Incredible," Henrietta breathed.

"Isn't that too modern for this box?" Ralph asked.

"Actually, combination locks were used as early as the 1870s if you can believe it. This one does seem to align with the 1960s date that I've come up with. But now I'm stuck."

"I assume it will only accept the proper combination," Henrietta asked.

"We could just smash it open."

"No!"

"No!"

Henrietta and Olivia responded at the same time and with the same ferocity.

"All right, all right," Ralph said, holding up his hands. "I'll take smashing off the table."

"It's a *very* expensive box, Mister Gershwin. We would be fools to destroy it."

"Does that mean you'll leave it unsolved rather than break into it?"

"Perhaps," Henrietta said, her head tilting to the side as it did when she was deep in thought. "But I have a few other options we can try first. Please remember to secure it in the safe when you're done with it, Olivia."

"Certainly," the young woman said.

Henrietta and Ralph left the small room and Ralph gently rested a hand on her shoulder to pull her to a stop. "I don't like you being here by yourself. It's clear from that note that someone is not happy you have that box in there. There's no telling what they'll do to get it."

"How did you know about the note?" she said, shocked. Then realization dawned. "You talked with your old buddy on the force, didn't you?"

Ralph's guilty look was all she needed to see.

"I'll be fine. I have that security system you *insisted* I install, and it likely scared away whoever had attempted to come in."

Even as she said the words, she wasn't convinced. The whole thing had seemed too planned. The note under the door. No locks or glass broken. Even the feeling she'd had of someone watching her find the note stuck out to her. Of course she shared none of this with Ralph. There was no need to have him worry any more than he already was.

His eyes were narrowed, and she could see that he disagreed. "All right then," he said, though she knew it wasn't an agreement. It was more a 'we'll see who's right and it's going to be me' look.

"All right," she said too brightly as she headed toward the room she'd been dusting in. "I'll see you bright and early tomorrow for the front lawn set up."

"See you then," he said, his broad shoulders turning away from her and making a path down the antique-lined hallway to the front door.

Part of her felt guilty for not sharing her next move with him, but the other reason was that she was much less likely to look suspicious if she went back to the house where the auction had been than if she brought along a private investigator. This way, she'd keep it to the antique business all while asking a few, very pertinent questions.

The game was most certainly afoot.

7

The sun reflected off the water, making Henrietta think of a lighthouse she'd visited as a girl. The large, reflecting disc had been so bright she'd thought she'd gone blind after one quick glimpse. Thankful when her sight returned moments later, Henrietta had remembered that incident down to the last detail.

Lighthouses were still something that she loved. There was a beauty to the steadfastness of the keeper, the importance of the light, and the romance of a beacon on a hill that warned sailors away from impending doom.

The sound of her Mini Cooper's tires grinding on the gravel of the drive brought her thoughts back to the present.

In the confusion of the threatening email and then the subsequent alarm triggering, Henrietta had almost forgotten Millicent Bedford's informational email until that morning. She'd browsed through her account when she came to the unopened email and nearly smacked herself on the forehead. Here was a wealth of information she'd all but ignored because she'd allowed herself to be flustered.

Never let circumstances outweigh your good judgement. Her mother's saying came back to her and she nodded. She'd let her circumstances outweigh more than just her judgement, they had taken over her thoughts and created a type of tunnel vision. That was simply unacceptable.

Her sensible flats crunched against the gravel and then tap-tapped on the refinished wood steps of the old-turned-new house. While the renovations still bothered her, she'd discovered through Millicent's overly-investigative information that the man who was overseeing the remodel was also the man who had arranged the estate sale.

A chime that sounded more like waterfall over pebbles echoed on the other side of the ultra-modern door and Henrietta turned her attention to the slice of sea she could make out in the distance. If they hadn't ruined the house with their modern eye, she might have considered buying the place.

"Uh, hello?"

Caught in her thoughts once again, Henrietta put on a smile and turned to the man who stood in the doorway. He was tall in the way studious men who cared more about books than brawn were. His shoulders created a dramatic cut in the doorway while the rest of him was covered in expensive style. Dark slacks. Dark coat. Brilliantly white shirt. His glasses reminded Henrietta of the remodeled house. Too new to be on a face that old.

"Ah yes, hello. My name is Henrietta Hewitt. I own H.H. Antiques in town."

"Hello, Miss Hewitt. I'm Chesterton Mallory." He scrunched up his forehead, no doubt trying to remember if he had dealings with her he'd forgotten about.

"I've come to ask a few questions regarding an item I purchased here at the estate sale as well as some historical questions. I hear you're the man to answer those inquiries?"

His lips slipped into a thin line that mirrored the horizon. "I'm afraid I don't know much."

"That's all right," she said, taking a step forward. "I'll take what I can get."

"Then please, come in." Everything in his countenance screamed that he'd rather she leave, but apparently, his courtesy won out over his personal desires and he stepped aside, letting her into the foyer.

"I'm assuming you saw the interior when you were here for the auction."

"Yes," she said, her tone dropping. "It's a shame."

"Excuse me?"

Not one to mince words, Henrietta gave him a rundown of the gross misinterpretations of the

Victorian style the 'repairs' created, ending with, "Should I have been consulted, this would have been preserved in style as well as historical accuracy. Down the road, if this is difficult to sell, that may affect its future."

Mr. Mallory was taken aback by her bluntness but recovered with a fake smile. "We're confident that someone will see what a gem this old house is and be inspired to purchase it based on the *new life* we've infused into it."

"New life does not have to come at the sake of old charm. Alas, it's a moot point since the deed has been done. Now…" She clasped her hands together. "Let's talk about Mister Gerald Patton."

"Please, this way," he said, directing her to a sunroom with an incredible cliff-side view. "What would you like to know?"

"First off, did you have any threats before the auction?"

"Threats?" Chesterton looked at her with the first real show of authenticity. "No, nothing like that. Mister Patton's estate was highly treasured, and we had many fine bidders—yourself included—show up for the auction."

"Since I've purchased the puzzle box, I've received two threats."

"I assure you that our list of purchasers is *not* made public, and we are not in any way responsible for—"

"I'm not going to sue you. I promise," she said with a

smile. "I just need to know more about why this box might be so important. Do you know anything of its history?"

Chesterton leaned back in the settee he had directed them to and stared into the distance for a moment. "I hired a small team, people I usually work with on estate sales, and they did an excellent job of culling the information and prepping the rooms and such with sale items. I didn't really oversee the individual sell-sheets and whatnot since they already were."

"Of course, the sign of a well-delegated system."

"However," he said, a light coming into his eyes, "I do know of a box of personal affects that was left here. I believe some of my researchers used it to help date things, but I doubt they went through all of it. There just wasn't time. I don't think it would hurt if you took a look through the box."

"Why, Mister Mallory, that would be spectacular."

He beamed at her praise. "I don't mind helping you one bit, Miss Hewitt. Just be certain that what you observe is not damaged in any way or divulged to the press without first talking to me."

It was an odd thing to say, as if he assumed she would find something noteworthy, but perhaps that was the way Mr. Mallory had become accustomed to working. Everything was a potential story, something to be sold or publicized on social media.

"You have my word. Now where's the box?"

It had been nearly three hours and, while Henrietta had found many fascinating things in the box of papers and photographs, nothing led her to an answer regarding the puzzle box. There was one last sheaf of papers to look through before she tossed in the towel.

She pulled out an old flex file folder and fanned it out. The documents seemed to be split into alphabetical categories, so she pulled out the first one. It had a receipt for Acme Flooring dated from the sixties. These were receipts from the house.

Hope sparked in her chest and she tried to remember the name of the designer that Olivia had said created the box. Then it came to her: Salvatore Green. Would it be under his name, or had he worked as part of a company?

On the off chance he, as a designer, would want to go by his name, she looked in the G section. A few papers in, she struck gold. An invoice for the box denoted its creation date in the sixties just as Olivia had discovered. At the top, a rusted staple held the remaining corner of a paper that had rested behind the invoice.

Below, on the yellowing page, she could just make out a note written in a slanted script: *Created per specifications. Compartments and code to specifications.*

That correlated with what they'd already discovered, but what were the specifications and what was the code? Had it been part of the paper behind? If so, when was it removed and where was it now?

It was maddening not to know the combination. She already knew from Olivia's research that there were almost ten thousand combinations possible with a four-number lock. They wouldn't guess it any time soon, though she had given Olivia a few suggestions for combinations based on her observations at the house and of the man.

"Looks like you've found something," Chesterton said, coming into the room. "What is it with that file folder?"

"What do you mean?"

"I'd almost forgotten until seeing that folder, but we had another bidder come to look in that box a few weeks ago. Just before the auction, actually. She wanted to see the items early, but I told her that was simply not possible. She was a nosey one, though."

"How so?"

"I found her wandering around upstairs when I had *clearly* left her down here where you are. She said she was just admiring the beauty of the house, but I didn't feel comfortable with that. I asked her to leave as I had other business to attend to and she went without any problem."

"What did she look like?"

"Oh, I don't know. Young. Dark hair. Large glasses."

Henrietta formed an image in her mind. "An accent?"

"No. Not really. Perhaps from somewhere on the East Coast."

"Interesting."

"What did you find there?"

"The original bill of sale for the item I purchased. Would it be possible to have this?"

Chesterton took it and looked over the information. "Seeing as how it pertains to the item you purchased, I see no problem in giving you this. It likely would have come with the papers you got had this been found. Clearly good help is hard to find," he said, rolling his eyes.

"Thank you for your help, Mister Mallory. You've been a joy to work with."

He offered a tightlipped smile that almost reached his eyes and turned to lead her out. On the porch, Henrietta turned toward him. "I have one last question."

"Yes?"

"Do you know of any place near here that is hiring? Or perhaps renting?"

His eyebrows hiked. "Are you looking to move to The Cliffs?" he asked, referring to the term the neighbored went by.

"Not exactly."

"I haven't heard of anything like that, but if I do, I would be happy to let you know."

She offered him her card and bid him good day. While her time had been somewhat successful, it hadn't delivered the information she'd hoped for. She'd thought perhaps to find a slip of paper with the combination on it—likely wishful thinking—but the receipt would have to do. She'd turn it over to Olivia and see what she could find out about it.

Henrietta pulled out onto the main highway but slammed on her brakes when a young girl in capris and a bright blue tank top barely managed to swerve out of her way. She'd been riding her bike across the two-lane highway headed for a trail that Henrietta knew ran by the highway and down to the water.

The woman drew Henrietta's glance and she noted dark hair that was pulled back in a pony-tail. She managed to turn onto the path and all Henrietta could see was her profile, but it made Henrietta gasp.

She would have sworn that it was Cybil Markham.

8

"Why didn't you stop her?" Ralph said, coming around from behind his desk in the cramped two-room office space he rented for the Gershwin Private Investigators workspace.

"Oh sure, drive my car off the road and chase after a young woman asking if she's the same girl who tried to disappear?"

Ralph rolled his eyes. "More like, ask her if she *is* that very woman, but minus the chasing."

"She was on a bike."

"Don't you jog in the mornings?"

"Not for twenty years."

Ralph harrumphed. "Well, there's a lead down the drain."

"Hardly," Henrietta pointed out. "We know that she's still in town despite leaving that terrible motel, and we know that she's in the area of The Cliffs."

"Speaking of that, how is she affording that?"

"I've got a theory on that."

"Oh, do you now? Care to enlighten me?"

"Not quite yet."

Ralph showed his obvious frustration, but she ignored him.

"What *can* you enlighten me on?"

"The fact that she is definitely here for a reason."

"We established that."

"Yes, but I think it has to do with something on The Cliffs. Maybe even the Patton house. I'll have Olivia look into it. See you tomorrow morning?"

Ralph stared at her. "You're really not going to tell me more than that?"

"Not yet," she said in a singsong voice as she turned to head out the front door. She almost ran into Scott. "Hello."

"Hiya, Henrietta."

"See you tomorrow morning?"

"Bright and early. Livi texted me."

"Oh, did she now?" Henrietta managed to keep her smile in check. "Good. I'm grateful for your help."

"Any time."

She lifted a hand in farewell and left out of the front door.

The sun drenched the landscape in an unusually warm day and Henrietta had a wild notion to go to the rocky beach she sometimes frequented when things were slow. But things were certainly *not* slow. In fact, she'd neglected much of her duties for the Blackberry Festival while helping Ralph with this missing person case and she was beginning to feel the strain of stress in making sure she'd be ready for their lawn prep the next day.

Just two days until the festival began and—

"Miss Hewitt!" The overly bright tone of the voice portended an exaggerated conversation with the fretful Mayor Lawrence.

"Hello and good-bye, Ricky," she said with a wave and a smile, climbing into her Mini. "I'm off to the shop for last minute preparations."

"I know, I know, but—" With moves faster than Henrietta would have attributed to such a slight, pale man, he caught her door before it could close. "Just one last *verbal* confirmation on your entry for the silent auction."

Verbal. As if their five-page contract wasn't valid enough.

"Yes, of course. What would make you think otherwise?"

"This nonsense about a break-in at your place associated with this trinket. It *is* just a trinket, isn't it? You said it was worth a lot, but then you called it a toy. It's all very confusing. Am I correct in assuming it's all just a fluke then?"

She had used the word trinket, to her detriment, and now she had to face a few facts with the man. In all actuality, it was better to get this over with now.

"I do have an auction item, per our written agreement—" She couldn't help but throw that in. "—but it's not exactly as stated in the agreement."

His eyes went wide with terror and his cheeks paled, if that were possible. "I—I—" he sputtered.

"Not to worry though, there are only a few provisos that we'll need to alter."

"A few…alter…" He blinked so rapidly she was afraid his eyelashes may float away.

"I'll be providing security for the box and—"

"*Security?*" He held up a hand and took in a deep breath. "You must tell me exactly what is going on, Miss Hewitt."

No matter how many times she'd insisted that he call her Henrietta, he hadn't caved, and she was fairly certain he never would.

"The rumors you heard about the break-in do seem to be somewhat centralized around the box. But that's all right, I'll have Ralph there to watch over it the whole time it's on display."

"Ralph? Shouldn't we get someone with a gun?"

Henrietta laughed despite herself. "What makes you think he *doesn't* have a gun? And besides, I don't want it to look like the item is dangerous. It's only the people—or person—trying to get to it that worries me."

"Oh, *sure*," he said, his sarcasm evident. "What is it about this…this item that is so special? Are you certain it will bring a good price?"

"I've no doubt in its validity or its worth. Now

please, I really must go and see to the multitude of things on my lists of preparations for tomorrow. Good day, Mayor Lawrence."

Ricky looked as if he were considering standing in front of her car until he gained more satisfactory answers from her, but he stepped aside and let her back up.

She was glad, because she wasn't sure she was prepared to answer all that he might ask. Yes, she was confident that the box was wanted, but was it because of someone's observed importance or was it the creator of the box and his artistry that drew the attraction?

She hoped that Olivia would be able to shed some light on the whole endeavor, seeing as they still had much to uncover about the puzzle box, including the secret four-number code.

Ralph and Scott showed up bright and early, Olivia not far behind with a bag of pastries from the bakery at the south end of town where she lived.

"I got you a bear claw because I knew you love those," she said, offering it to Scott.

"Did you get me a croissant?" Ralph asked, hopeful.

"Um," she said, biting her lip.

"She might not have, but I did." Henrietta handed

over a bag from *Espresso Yourself* and Ralph's grin spread like wildfire.

"Ain't you the sweetest, Henri?"

Henrietta rolled her eyes and began doling out responsibilities with the ease and skill of a military general. When her minions had finished their breakfast and between sips of coffee, they began to cart out the heavy antique furniture into the designated spots in the yard.

The tent company had set up their large white tent that spanned both sides of the walking path, and Henrietta was happy to see that it felt light and airy underneath the awning. It would give it a bit of an old world feeling, and she thought that very appropriate for an antique shop.

"Did you say you wanted this on the left or the right side?" Ralph asked, carrying an ornately carved side table with matching marble top. Scott stood behind him with the table top, his lean muscles straining. He likely had the heavier piece out of the two.

"I didn't, but…" She considered both sides.

"Any minute now," Ralph said with a grunt.

"Oh, stop. You don't hear your son complaining, and he's carrying *stone*." She looked to her left and pointed. "There."

Olivia came down the steps with a hatbox in one hand and a valise in the other. "I think these will do well for the photobooth. You sure it's all right for people to be touching these?"

"Yes. I went through the selection of vintage clothing we have, and I think these will be just fine. They aren't my expensive pieces and if they were ruined, it wouldn't be the end of the day. Not that I'd *like* them to be ruined."

"Of course not."

"You may want to keep those inside until tomorrow though, right?" Scott said, coming up to them. He reached for the hatbox, pulling off the lid and grinning. "Wouldn't want any ruffians coming in here and messing around with priceless antiques." He proceeded to take the hat out of the box and plopped it on his head, pretending to adjust it to get the best angle.

"No, we certainly wouldn't want that," Olivia said with a girlish giggle. She went to reach for the hat, but Scott backed up straight into Ralph.

"Watch it, son." Ralph eyed the ornate hat adorned with netting and feathers. An eyebrow arched. "It's not your color."

"It's black!"

"Exactly."

They all shared a laugh and Scott gingerly lifted the hat from his head. "You're right. It would look much better on…" He tilted his head, assessing Olivia, before placing it gently on her short bob. "Livi here."

She blushed, the deep crimson color spreading across her pale cheeks, and Henrietta shot a look at Ralph.

"Yeah, definitely better," Ralph said, completely oblivious to anything other than the facts.

"Olivia?"

The four of them turned as one to the newcomer walking up the steps.

"N-Nelson." Olivia reached up to tug the hat off. "What are you doing here?"

"Came to see if we were still on for lunch." He eyed the hat, pushing up his wire-rimmed glasses with his index finger. "Why do you have that dreadful hat on? Makes you look ridiculous."

This time, Olivia's cheeks were stained in embarrassment. "It's for the photobooth."

"How are things over at Greenfield?" Ralph asked.

"Oh, you know, better than the private investigation sector, I'd wager." He laughed, the sound nasally, and Henrietta looked from her assistant to Scott then finally back to Nelson Stern. The young man didn't seem to have much awareness of social circumstances.

"Now, now, Mister Stern," she said, "no need to compare. All our fields of work are successful in their own ways."

"Sure, just some more so than others." Nelson leveled his gaze at Scott. Henrietta knew that the two had gone to high school together and that there had been some kind of divide. Wasn't there always in high school? Scott, being a talented, athletic young man had done well in football whereas Nelson had focused more on the sciences, computer science to be specific.

Born where rivalries begin and cemented by circumstances unique to small towns, their high school dislike had stayed with them despite the years past.

"You'll kindly let us go back to work, Mister Stern," she said, pushing him firmly toward the front gate. "You'll have Olivia to yourself for an hour in a little less than four hours. That should be sufficient. Good morning."

He stumbled on the first step and turned to wave. "I'll pick you up. We're doing Greek!" Then he disappeared.

Olivia let out a sigh. "I hate Greek," she muttered before heading back into the shop for another box of items for the photobooth.

"I'll go, uh, help her." Scott followed her, and Henrietta shook her head.

"Young love," she said, her gaze on Scott's back.

"What was *that* all about?" Ralph said, adjusting a chair to be more in line with the others near it.

"If you can't see it, then you're more blind than I thought."

"Hey, what does—"

"Hello, hello, lovely people!" His question was broken off by the appearance of Sassy Roberts at the front gate.

"Sassy!" Henrietta rushed toward her, arms outstretched. "You'd better have brought me my orders!"

Sassy grinned and nodded. "In the car. Ralph, be a dear and go grab the box that's marked with H.H."

"Yes, ma'am," he said, plodding by them.

"This looks lovely," the older woman said. She had short, gray hair atop a round face that matched her somewhat round physique. She always said that a thin sweets-maker was not to be trusted, and Henrietta wouldn't disagree with her. The confections that came from her shop proof enough of her talent.

"You know I'd be happy to give you discounts when you do orders like this," Sassy said, finally turning away from the furniture.

"That would defeat the purpose. Besides, I couldn't celebrate the Blackberry Festival without blackberry treats. You provide that, and I may or may not shamelessly tout your amazing shop."

Sassy grinned like a proud parent. "We small businesses have to stick together, that's for sure. But..." She pulled her gaze from a gilded mirror she was admiring. "I heard a rumor about a break-in. Is it true, Hen?"

Sassy was one of only a handful of people who called her Hen and got away with it. "It's true, but no need to worry. Nothing was taken." She wanted to say she was fairly certain that the whole purpose of the ordeal had been a scare tactic, but that wouldn't reassure her friend.

"But surely you're not still staying here while the culprit is on the loose!"

DANIELLE COLLINS

"There isn't any reason to think they'll come back," she said, though not fully believing it herself. "Besides, my alarm works fine—evidenced by the other night—so I'll be fine."

Sassy shook her head. "I know Hal is not the most terror-inducing image, but you're welcome to stay with us. He'd move heaven and earth to see you safe. Sometimes I think he cares more for you than me," she said with an overexaggerated laugh.

"You know that's not true," Henrietta said, laughing. She had known Hal, Sassy's grouchy but inwardly sweet husband, had taken a liking to Henrietta from day one. He gave her a hard time, but it was all in the name of friendship.

"Well, the offer stands. Anyway, I must run." Ralph stepped to the gate, bending under the weight of the box Sassy was delivering. "He's a keeper," she said with a wink over her shoulder as she opened the gate for him then disappeared.

"This thing weighs a ton!"

"Good thing there's only one box." She told him where to place it inside and surveyed the area. It looked ready, mostly, for the guests she'd entertain over the weekend for the Blackberry Festival. But was she ready for exhibiting the puzzle box, despite the warnings? And was she ready to face another possible break-in where there was actual damage? Only time would tell.

9

A night of fitful tossing and turning had left Sepia grouchy and napping in the sun on an 18th century divan and Henrietta feeling foggy. She'd already downed a latte from next door, but the fog hadn't cleared. Sassy's worry had somehow gotten to her and, while she wasn't one prone to imagination in the negative, she'd seen all sorts of ways that someone could have broken in to get at the puzzle box.

Thankfully, none of those things had come to pass, but now on the morning of the Blackberry Festival, she wasn't at her best. Thankfully, Olivia would be joining her to help deal with potential customers and the ones who always thought they knew more about history and antiques than those whose job it was to know the truth behind an object.

One last check that the puzzle box was indeed still in the safe left Henrietta sure of its safety and more aware of her own situation. Would Ralph truly be able to guard it? Would someone try and take it while it was on display?

At about three in the morning, she'd come up with an idea for that issue, though. She'd taken a photo of the box perched on a black velvet stand early that morning and used their laser jet printer to print out an archival quality print that she then mounted on a stiff board. She would allow the puzzle box to be viewed at the very beginning of the auction for those serious bidders, and then she would replace the actual box with the image and a statement that anyone could request to see the box in person if they so desired.

That would at least give her the upper hand, or so she hoped. Anyone who requested to see the box could be run through a quick check of their background and personhood, giving her information she wouldn't have otherwise.

It helped to have a plan, but she still worried that someone might take the opportunity of its being on display early on. That was something she'd have to leave in Ralph's care, though.

The grandfather clock chimed eight o'clock and she set about the preparations for moving most of her daily activity outside. She'd set up a small desk near the gate and would be able to watch all comers and goers as they came up to the antique shop. The front gate would be open, but there was no easily accessible back exit, so she felt confident in leaving most of the interior open.

She had a plate of blackberry scones, a tray of dark chocolate and blackberry from Sassy's shop, and blackberry lemonade she would set out for her guests, hoping to entice them in as much as to support her favorite local shops.

While the street would be closed off at both ends and shops would soon bring out their awnings to move into the street to sell their wares, Henrietta always opened early. It was her tradition. She had a few regulars she could count on to come browsing through her discounted sections in hopes of selling off a few pieces she'd had longer than she'd like. These customers always came early and tended to be regulars through the year. They tried to get her to divulge what pieces would be on sale at the festival, but she was as rigid as a schoolmarm's ruler when it came to giving away things like that. She liked to think they appreciated her resolve.

The scent of blackberry pancakes wafted toward her and she knew that the bakery was already preparing for the pancake eating contest and subsequent pancake breakfast that would take place in an hour.

For a moment—just a moment—Henrietta sat back and closed her eyes. She felt the familiarity of it all surround her. While she'd never brought out this many antiques in such a fashion, it still felt like years past. The nostalgia of it all was comforting, and she was almost able to forget that someone didn't want her to give up that puzzle box. Did that also mean that they knew the combination?

Her eyes shot open as the familiar sound of the creaking gate drew her back to the present. "Morning, Henrietta," Olivia said. She wore a linen jumper the color of denim over a bright pink shirt and topped off the outfit with large gold hoop earrings.

"You look lovely this morning," Henrietta said. "Ready for a busy day?"

"I wore my comfortable sandals," she said, pointing to the sandals with yoga mat material cushions for soles.

"That was a brilliant idea."

"Anyone come in yet?" she asked, setting her coffee on their makeshift desk.

"Not yet. I just opened up, though. You know how it is—that pancake eating contest takes up a lot of the focus. Oh, wait," she laughed, "you *don't* know how it is. I'm sorry, dear, I keep forgetting this is your first time to our illustrious Blackberry Festival."

Olivia smiled. "I like that you forget I'm not a local." She took in a deep breath and let out a deep sigh. "I love all of this. The excitement, the commotion, all of it."

"We'll talk again this evening," Henrietta said with a grin.

"I know it'll be a lot of work. I hear people come from hundreds of miles to see this festival! But I think my excitement will get me through."

"I do hope so."

Olivia was just turning to put her lunch in the refrigerator when Henrietta's phone rang. She didn't recognize the number but waved Olivia on as she answered. "Hello, H.H. Antiques. This is Henrietta speaking."

"Ah, yes, Miss Hewitt." The voice sounded familiar and she tried to place it. "This is Chesterton Mallory over at the Patton house."

"Oh yes, good morning, Mister Mallory. What can I do for you?"

"Actually, it's what I can do for *you*." He paused for dramatic effect and she waited for him to continue. "Right, well, you'd asked about the goings on here at The Cliff's and I did hear from someone a few houses down—toward the east, that is—who said they'd recently hired a new house member. She came with a recommendation from the owner's personal friend and they hired her on the spot."

"Oh, that is good news. What house is it, if I may ask?"

"Certainly. The Wilshire Estate. Not quite as progressive as Patton House, but—"

"Yes, I know it."

"My contact is Francine Dubois." He said her last name with a thick and overexaggerated French accent, and Henrietta had to try to keep her smile from her voice.

"Lovely. Would you mind sending over her contact information to me via my email?"

"Certainly. And, Miss Hewitt," he added, his voice dropping, "Francine said the young girl has been missing since yesterday."

This news came as a shock. "Missing?"

"Yes. It was all anyone could talk about at our staff lunch. Apparently, she's all but disappeared."

"Have they called the police?"

He hesitated. "Not exactly. You see, the Wilshire has some…questionable hiring policies."

Henrietta understood at once. Some of the estates on The Cliffs were known for hiring illegal immigrants and paying them under the table. Why they did this, she could only guess, but mostly it came down to the appearance of wealth juxtaposed to the *reality* of it.

"I see."

"You didn't hear this from me, but they didn't have any papers on her, no proof to her identity, and she only left behind a pair of black gloves and a few toiletries. Nothing too personal."

"Well, thank you for sharing this with me. I'll be looking in to it."

"Please, don't mention my name…"

"Don't you worry, Mister Mallory, my lips are sealed."

The evening was quickly approaching, and Henrietta felt her exhaustion deep to her bones. It was only the first day of the festival, but already she was looking for the rest at the end of it.

The auction was starting in less than forty-five minutes, and Ralph had already taken the box, Scott assisting him for extra security, to the tent. They would stand guard near it, but Ralph had also alerted his buddies on the police force to keep an eye out.

She knew that her worry was for naught, a criminal would have no means of escape even if they got close enough to pilfer the box, but still...she didn't want it leaving her hands without first cracking the four-digit code.

After locking the front door of the shop, she pulled her purse strap over her shoulder and tucked her lightweight sweater over the strap. The square dance competition would begin soon as well, and she wanted to catch some of her friends who danced competitively. She also wanted to watch those watching the puzzle box. It would be a busy night for her.

The streets were clear though still closed, the EZ-up tents zipped up tight for the night, but there was still an atmosphere of celebration. The excitement would be taking place in the town circle area. It was the hub of four streets that, rather than form a corner, the city had put in a traffic circle and used the center to make a space for just such a celebration. It was part park, part meeting place, and part heart of the city of

Heart's Grove. They called it Heart Park and no matter the season, the Ladies Auxiliary had the central gazebo decorated accordingly.

As Henrietta approached the town circle, she saw the large tent where the silent auction was taking place. The items would be displayed today and tomorrow, and bidders would write down their bids accordingly on the sheets provided. She also saw food trucks lining one side, the paved area where the square dance competition was just about to begin, and other fun game areas for children and adults alike.

The whole area was strung with bistro lights and gave off the atmosphere of family and fun. She paused for a moment at the mouth of an alley, enjoying the scene before her. She had lost track of how many Blackberry Festivals she'd taken part in or attended, but she knew that she never wanted to miss one. To miss this sight would be a travesty.

Just then, the sound of something—or someone— kicking a trashcan behind her made Henrietta turn. A nervous feeling crept up her spine, tingling a path to the base of her neck.

"Hello?" she called out. Her mind immediately went to whoever had broken into her antique shop, but she doubted anyone would try something when she was so close to a large crowd of people. She was certainly within shouting distance.

Another sound of rattling drew Henrietta deeper

into the alley. It was foolish, but she'd never shied away from a mystery. "Hello? Is someone there?"

A sniff. Then another sound of scuffling. There was definitely someone hiding behind the garbage cans at the back of the small Italian Bistro.

In three purposeful strides, she was looking down at a young woman with dark hair pulled back into a ponytail.

"You must be Cybil Markham. Why were you following me?"

The girl's eye grew wide and she pushed up to a standing position. "I, uh…"

"Come now, you must be hungry, and perhaps could use a shower? I think you've been on the streets a night, haven't you?"

"How—how did you know that?"

"Call it women's intuition," she said with a soft smile. "This way."

Part of Henrietta regretted missing the square dance competition and she had looked forward to observing those observing the puzzle box, but Ralph and Scott would bring it back to her safe that night so, until then, she decided to use her time a little differently than she'd anticipated.

"How do you know who I am?" the girl said as they retraced Henrietta's steps back toward her shop. "I'm not from around here."

"Let's just say I freelance with a private investigator who your parents hired to find you."

"My…parents." The way the girl said it drew Henrietta's interest.

"They seem to be very worried about you," she mused.

"Mmm." The girl didn't elaborate.

"If I may ask, why did you come to Heart's Grove?" Cybil opened her mouth to respond, but her stomach let out a furious growl that was audible from several feet away. "Never mind that just yet. We'll get you some food and *then* you can tell me what I'm sure is a fascinating tale."

The young woman looked grateful but also a little hesitant. When they reached the antique shop, Henrietta took Cybil upstairs and showed her to the guest bathroom where the plush towels were clean and just waiting for a guest.

"I'll be in the kitchen when you're done. Just down this hall and to the right."

"Thank you, Missus…"

"Miss Hewitt. But Henrietta will do just fine."

"Thank you, Henrietta."

Henrietta went to the kitchen and pulled out supplies to make dinner. She didn't have much on hand since she'd planned on eating at a festival food truck, but she managed to pull together a decent plate of spaghetti and vegetables with a light marinara sauce by the time the young woman emerged from the shower.

"That smells amazing."

"I usually offer any sort of pasta with bread, but I'm afraid I don't have any on hand."

The girl sat down, and Henrietta slid a steaming plate in front of her.

"This is *perfect*." She wasted no time digging in and Henrietta joined her with her own plate. They chewed in silence for a few minutes until it looked as if Cybil was finally ready to talk.

10

"I came to Heart's Grove because of my grandfather."

"Grandfather?" Henrietta was surprised. Ralph hadn't mentioned any other family.

"Yes. Gerald Patton."

"Gerald…" Henrietta nodded. "I see."

"I didn't get to see him much growing up, but I did come out here one year when I was ten. I spent six weeks of the summer with him in that house, and it was the best six weeks of my life." Cybil's eyes shimmered with a sheen of tears.

"Go on, dear," Henrietta said, gently patting the girl's hand.

"I went back to New York after that but vowed I'd come back as soon as I could. Grandpa is…was—" She swallowed. "—a grump, but he really wasn't deep down. He liked me and said I could come back any time."

"So, why didn't you?"

"For a number of reasons, most being my...parents."

Again, there was something in the way the girl talked about her parents that felt off to Henrietta, but before she could ask, Cybil was speaking again.

"I finally managed to save up enough money on my own and decided I was going to do it—I was coming west. Even bought a ticket on my lucky day, the tenth of July. By then I'd heard about my grandfather's sickness and thought I could stay with him. You know, nurse him back to health. Then the next day, I found out that he had died. It was so...sudden. It felt impossibly fast. By then though, I'd already purchased a ticket and I was going back on my promise to myself."

"So, you came out here without any plans in place aside from a bus ticket?"

"Sort of." She shrugged. "Honestly, I had hoped that I could stay at grandpa's when I got here, but I spoke with someone who was managing the estate—"

"Mister Mallory?"

"No," she said, shaking her head. "I can't remember what his name was, but he said that without proper identification, I couldn't even look at the will."

"Interesting."

"Of course I didn't have my birth certificate with me and..." She dropped her gaze.

"What is it, Cybil?" Henrietta prodded.

"My mom was not exactly an...approved member of the Patton family."

"I see," And Henrietta was beginning to.

"She never got along with Grandpa Patton and, while I believe I am in the will, I think he put me under the name Cybil *Patton.* Not Cybil Markham."

"And you can't seem to establish the correlation between the two. I see. Can't your mother help?"

"That's where things get…hairy."

Henrietta was now fully intrigued by the complexity of this case. "In what way?"

"To make a long story a bit shorter, when my mother was eighteen, she fell in love and got pregnant."

"Let me guess, that child was you?"

"Exactly. She didn't marry my father, Paul Markham, who was just some fisherman she never saw again after that summer, but it was enough for my grandfather to send her away that fall to a friend of his in New York. You know, to save him the shame and all of that. Well, while she was there, she met and fell in love with another guy—my stepdad, George Stone. I decided to take my real father's last name, even though I never met him."

"And your grandfather didn't approve of him either?"

"No, and for good reason. George is a conman."

Henrietta's eyes widened.

"Anyway, my mom died a year ago from cancer—" Cybil's eyes dropped again. "—and George remarried about six months after that."

"Rather fast, isn't it?"

"That's what I said." Cybil bit her lip, looking into the distance for a moment. "It's all a big mess, but basically, both of my parents are *not* my parents and I don't trust either of them."

"Sounds like you have good reason for that," Henrietta agreed. "But now you're here, and your parents are looking for you because…"

"I honestly don't know. When you told me that, it shocked me because, to be honest, they haven't shown a shred of care toward me. My stepfather maybe cared about me when I was younger. I mean, he was the only dad I knew, but once mom started getting sick years before she passed, he stopped showing as much interest in our lives."

"I'm sorry to hear all of this, Cybil," Henrietta said.

"Thanks. I just don't know what to do. It's clear that my grandfather left me *something* in the will, I just don't know what and I don't know how to get it."

Henrietta was quiet for a long time, but finally, she met Cybil's gaze with an assessing one of her own. "Why do you think your 'parents' are so interested in finding you?"

Cybil looked down. "I'd say it was to get the money back I used for bus fare, but that's long gone. They'd do anything for a buck, though."

"Yes, I see."

The doorbell rang, scaring them both. "Ah, that will be my friend—the private investigator."

"He can't know I'm here," Cybil said, jumping up. "I

can't let my parents know where I am. Not until I can stand to be on my own."

"You're eighteen, are you not?"

"They won't care. They'll drag me back to New York on some pretense that I stole money from them. Please," she begged Henrietta with soulful eyes.

Henrietta didn't want to be in the middle of this. In fact, if she had her way, she'd be as far from all of this as she could possibly get, but that was no longer possible.

"We'll see what to do, but for now, go ahead and stay in the spare bedroom across the hall from the bathroom you used."

"Thank you," she said, giving Henrietta a quick coconut shampoo-scented hug before dashing down the hall.

What was she getting herself into?

"Thanks for breakfast," Ralph said, reaching for the last blackberry scone on a plate in the breakroom of H.H. Antiques.

"Good thing I had Olivia bring more over from the bakery," she observed.

He merely grinned while he bit into it.

"I asked you to come here for a reason," she said, sending an impulsive look up the stairs before refocusing on Ralph. "I'm afraid you're not going to be too happy with me."

He pulled his eyes away from the last few bites of the scone. "What does that mean?"

Henrietta had tossed and turned—again—most of the night, worrying about the girl asleep down the hall. When the clock finally struck six, she sent a message to Ralph asking him to come over as soon as he could, making sure to state it wasn't urgent.

He'd come just a little after seven and now she had to share what she'd discovered from his missing person. She also had to somehow convince him not to tell the people who had hired him that he'd found the girl they were looking for. Henrietta wasn't sure she even wanted to call Cybil their daughter at this point.

"Spit it out, Henri," he said, his brows dipping into a frown.

"Oh, Ralph," she said, tossing her hands up, "it's bit of a mess."

"Hey now," he said, coming around the counter and gripping her firmly, but gently at the shoulders. "Tell me what's going on."

"First, you have to promise me that you won't speak a word of this to anyone yet. Promise?"

"This sounds serious."

"Promise?" she repeated.

"Yeah, I promise."

"I found Cybil Markham."

"You what?" His voice was loud, and Henrietta

shushed him with another look upstairs. "Please don't tell me she is *upstairs* at this very moment. I swear, Henrietta, if you—"

"You said you wouldn't say anything. You promised!"

"That was before it was my *job* we were talking about! I'm in a contract with this girl's parents. They are worried sick and—"

"Just hold on a moment, let me explain a few things to you."

He looked like he wanted to argue but, true to his good nature, Ralph kept his mouth shut and nodded for her to continue. She explained the whole conversation she'd had with the girl the night before and how she was fairly certain that she was telling the truth. Probably.

"Your assurance is stunning," he said with dry humor.

"One can never truly know the mind of another. You know that just as well as I."

He sighed heavily. "I do. But you've got to let me talk with her."

"That's why I had you come over. I figured if you're already here when she wakes up, there won't be much chance that she'll disapprove of me calling you..."

"Sneaky," he observed, before continuing, "What do you think, though, honestly, Henri?" This time, Ralph's stare held no humor, only serious, deductive reasoning.

"I'm not sure what to think. She seems to be telling

the truth, though there is the chance she knows more than she's let on and she has yet to say what that is. But I don't think she's completely pulling the wool over our eyes."

"I trust your judgement. Let's see if we can't help the girl."

They tromped up the stairs, Ralph's heavy boots making much more racket than Henrietta would have approved of if he'd just been coming up to see her. Instead, she figured the noise could be a good way to wake up the girl. It was already past seven-thirty and, while it was still early and she wanted the girl to recover, she still wanted to figure this out as quickly as possible.

She also wanted to ask Cybil about the puzzle box, something she'd meant to do the night before but had forgotten in the midst of what Cybil had shared.

Knocking softly on the door, she called out, "Cybil? Sorry to bother you, dear. Cybil?"

There was no response and Henrietta frowned. She tried the handle, but it was locked. "Cybil? Is everything all right?" Still no response. "I hope she's all right!" she said to Ralph.

"Want me to kick in the door?"

Henrietta gasped. "Are you out of your mind! That door is original to this house. Men," she said, rolling her eyes as she slipped down the hallway to her room and came back with a key in hand. "Another good thing about the Victorian era, they made the best keys." She slipped the large, ornate key into the lock. The door opened quickly and silently on well-oiled hinges to reveal an empty room.

"She's gone."

The sheer curtains on the south-facing window fluttered in the soft sea breeze.

"Well, I'll be. She climbed out the window."

"We're on the second story!" Henrietta said, alarmed.

"Right, but…" Ralph stuck his head out of the window. "Yep. She just went out onto the roof, used the wisteria trellis, and poof. She's gone."

"I can't believe this."

"Now do you believe her?"

Henrietta shot him a look. "I'm not sure. I still believe at least some of what she was telling me is the truth."

"Right, but which parts?" He sent her a pointed look.

That was something she wouldn't be able to answer.

"I have an idea, though," Ralph said, rubbing at his stubbled jaw. "I'm going to ask Scott to look into that email you got."

"Why are we back on that email?"

"Because something isn't adding up and I'd like to know *what* that something is."

"What are you going to do about your clients?" she asked, worried at his reply.

He took in a breath, looking at her. "Seeing as how I

don't know where the girl is..." He held out his hands, indicating the room. "It looks like I've got nothing to report yet."

She beamed up at him. "For that, you can have an extra scone."

"That's what I was hoping," he said with a grin.

11

"Things are looking good," Scott said, looking at a 'sold' tag attached to the end of a nineteenth century fainting couch.

"Yes, I'd say things are going well for this year's festival," Henrietta agreed. She walked around the covered area, trailing her hand along some of her favorite pieces, most now sold. Thankfully, almost every person who had purchased a large item stationed on the lawn had agreed to wait until the festival was over to claim their items. With the exception of an eccentric older man who was just passing through for one day, her outdoor showcase was mostly untouched.

"I'm glad we've had all this out here," Olivia said, coming up with a stack of paper bags. "It makes it feel so welcoming and is really bringing people in to the main shop as well."

"Yes, I am happy with how things have been selling.

The teacups especially. Odd, but they are selling out like crazy!"

Scott shrugged. "Beats me as to why you'd want a teacup—it's gone in two gulps."

Both Henrietta and Olivia laughed, sharing a smile between them. "Have a tea party and you'll know why," Olivia said.

"No thanks." Scott wrinkled his nose, then turned to Henrietta. "Hey, could we talk inside real quick? My dad should be here any minute."

"Of course," Henrietta said, turning to Olivia. "Why don't we switch places for a bit. You've been caged up inside all morning."

"It's no problem, but yes. Let's switch. I'll be out here," she said, casting a sideways glance at Scott before moving to the register they'd set up outside.

"Follow me, Scott," Henrietta said, leading the way up the steps to the shop inside. She noticed that a few pieces had sold inside since that morning as well and she was beginning to feel even better about this year's festival. It wasn't so much the money coming in that she cared about, but she *did* want to make sure that what she had on hand was what the populace was interested in.

With the resurgence of vintage-inspired styles and 'retro fever,' as she termed it, Henrietta had seen major growth in the online portion of her business in addition to the in-shop purchases. Youth all the way up into Canada would come down and shop in her little antique haven, seeking out everything from vintage clothing to records and old cameras. She made certain to have things on hand that were major attractions in addition to the larger pieces of furniture that often sold to those restoring old houses.

"What's this all about?" she asked Scott when they reached the register at the heart of the shop.

"It's about what my dad called me to look into. I wasn't expecting to get a hit this soon, but—"

"A hit? So, then you *did* find something?"

He hesitated. "I really should wait for my dad."

"Yes. Of course. We both know he'll be sore if you spill the beans early."

He grinned, thankful that she understood, and pulled out his laptop. He set it on the counter and started typing away.

Henrietta helped a few customers looking for carnival glass before Ralph finally showed up.

"It's about time."

"I had to rescue a cat out of a tree."

"That's a new one," Henrietta mused.

"Actually, it's a very old one, and in this case, it happens to be true. Missus White let that black cat of hers hop up in the tree *again*. I swear the cat just does it for the attention."

"You'd never do anything like that," Henrietta crooned to Sepia atop the grandfather clock.

She licked her paw in response.

"So, what's this all about?"

"I did what you asked me—"

"Now that's a first."

"Dad." Scott gave his father a look and went back to his computer. "And I looked into the original pinging addresses from where the email was sent from."

"Hold up." Ralph held up his hand. "The what?"

"Suffice it to say..." Scott tapped a few keys, ignoring his father's question, and then turned the computer screen their way.

"That's Heart's Grove," Henrietta said, noticing the topography right away.

"And that—" Scott pointed out. "—is where the threatening email originated from."

She shrugged. "I mean, it *is* brilliant that you can narrow it down, but we had to assume that someone local was interested in getting the box."

"That's not all," Scott said. "I was...curious. Dad also told me about your guest."

"Ralph!" Henrietta chided.

"Hey. He's my son and my partner. He's got a right to know."

"Either way," Scott interrupted. "Look at this." He clicked another key and a separate bubble popped up very close to the first one.

"What are we seeing, son?"

Henrietta moved closer.

"That—" Scott said. "—is where the email to you about Cybil originated from."

"Wait, but..." Ralph looked up. "From Heart's Grove?"

"From the *same* computer."

Henrietta kept her gaze roaming over the people that surrounded her, Ralph by her side. The unsettling news about the origin of the emails—both to her and to Ralph—worried at the back of her mind, but they had a more pressing need. Find out where Cybil was.

"You think she'll be here?" Ralph whispered to Henrietta.

"I'm not sure, honestly." Henrietta worried her lip for a minute. She was kicking herself for not asking the girl about the puzzle box earlier.

It had been several hours since Cybil left the room at the house, and she and Ralph had devised a sort of plan. They would announce that they were bringing the puzzle box out for an hour for anyone who wanted to see it. As she'd thought it might, the anonymity of the box itself had drawn quite an interest from the crowd.

She'd heard snatches of conversation around her as she had looked at booths earlier during the day, and many people had said it contained treasure or a key to some secret place. It had made Henrietta want to laugh because she had no idea what it contained and wouldn't be able to tell anyone even if they asked, but no one was asking—merely speculating.

Now though, with Scott and Ralph having brought the box out of the safe and onto a small velvet pillow on a pedestal covered by a plexiglass shield Henrietta had used in her shop before, everyone oohed and ahhed around it as if it were the queen's jewels themselves.

"Isn't this a little risky?" Ralph asked.

"Not exactly." She did agree that there was the possibility someone might try something dramatic, but so far, nothing had happened. She also hadn't seen Cybil yet, which worried her.

There was no way to know if Cybil knew anything about the puzzle box and, since she hadn't had a chance to ask the girl about it, Henrietta could only guess as to what the girl would say. Had her grandfather shown her the box before? Was it possible she knew the code to open the combination lock? If she didn't know about it, then who was it that wanted the box?

"What's the bid up to?" Ralph asked.

"I'm not sure. I think the last time I looked, it was nearing one thousand."

"Wow." Ralph whistled low. "For that wooden box? It worth that much?"

"Beauty is in the eye of the beholder."

"So, I'll take that as a no."

"I wouldn't say that," she said with a cryptic smile. "But I will say that perhaps it's not the box itself that is worth so much to someone but the contents of the box that are so important."

"I'll say it again. Why don't we smash it and open it?"

"A few reasons, the least of them being decency to the artist." She shot him a pointed look. "There are some that say attempting to open a puzzle box by force can do a few things that we'd rather not risk. One being it could destroy whatever was inside. These puzzle makers were very adept at what they did and it's possible there could even be a small-scale explosive device waiting for us."

"No," Ralph said, not convinced.

"It would be rare, but it has happened in the past."

"Why else?" Ralph asked, and she could see the thought of danger did nothing to the man.

"Whatever is inside could be *part* of the box or puzzle."

"How so?"

"You saw the first piece and how it was removed, did you not?"

"Yep."

"If we get to the inner workings of the box, perhaps the numeric code releases a piece but it must be joined with another and another in turn. We'd never know the sequence if we simply smashed the thing open."

"Now that," Ralph said with a nod, "makes sense."

"Glad you approve." Her eyes had just passed over

the back corner when she thought she saw Cybil. "Ralph!"

"What?" he asked, following her stare.

"It looked like her. In that back corner."

"I'll go check it out."

She nodded but before he left, he leaned in close. "Don't you go anywhere."

She smiled her agreement and watched him skirt his way around the crowd. Scott was on the other side of the puzzle box and she was certain that he would be able to stop anyone should the need arise. But what about—

"Don't turn around. Come with me and don't make a scene." Something poked into her back and she let out a gasp of surprise.

"I will not—"

"If you don't want my partner back there to harm your precious private investigator, you'll do as I say. And remember, don't turn around."

Henrietta had a moment to weigh her options. Stay, make a scene, and create panic, or leave quietly with the person poking a gun into her back, hoping that she'd be able to alter the situation elsewhere.

"Fine."

His grip on her arm was like a vice. "Stop struggling."

Henrietta wanted to explain to the man that she didn't feel like being a lamb led to the slaughter, but she realized now was not the time. Instead, she allowed him to guide her toward the back of the area and out into the late afternoon sun.

He hesitated only a moment before walking around one of the food trucks and shoving her inside the back. It was a taco truck she hadn't seen before and all of the windows were closed. Was it *their* taco truck or had he simply seen an opportunity for privacy and taken it?

He released her and shoved her to a chair in the corner at the same time he pulled his extra-large hood down over his face. It had happened so quickly she hadn't even had a chance to see what he looked like.

"Modern conveniences," the man said, pointing to the hood. "Kids think they look cool. Criminals see them as an advantage."

Henrietta was disgusted, but she didn't want to anger her captor just yet. "Hmm," was all she said.

The next moment, the door opened, and a shorter person walked in, hood pulled down in the same way.

"You got her. Good."

The other person was clearly a woman, though her voice sounded lower than most, and Henrietta noticed how she stayed close to the man, almost in an intimate type of way.

"Yeah. You do your part?"

"Sure did," she said, laughing. Then she fell silent as she turned to face Henrietta. "Why wouldn't you do as we'd asked?"

"You mean in your threatening email? Why didn't I give in to fearmongering and threats? I think not."

"Oh, she sounds so hoity toity!" The woman made as if to advance toward Henrietta, but the man held her back.

"Not now." He turned back to Henrietta. "You're going to help us out."

Henrietta wanted to laugh but knew they were serious. "Oh? In what way will I do that?"

"You're going to get that puzzle box and bring it to us at San Juan Point tonight at midnight. No one with you, no cops."

"And why would I do that?"

The man's head tilted. "For many reasons, the first of which being that you're a decent person. The second being that, if you don't, Cybil's body is going to wash up on shore in a day or two and you'll feel really bad knowing you could have prevented her death."

Henrietta took in a deep breath at the man's words but remained calm. "I see."

"See, she's gonna do it. I told you she would."

"Hush," the man said. "Now, have we made ourselves clear?"

"Quite." Henrietta kept her eyes on where she assumed the man's eyes were. The next instant, the woman moved and pulled a bag over her head, and the world went black.

12

When Henrietta finally managed to make it out of the food truck, using one of the knives she'd seen attached to a magnetic strip at the back of the prep area to cut the intricately knotted rope that bound her wrists, she raced to the tent where she'd left Ralph.

"Where in the world were you?" he demanded, his anger melting the moment he recognized fear in her eyes. "What happened? Are you all right?"

She relayed everything that had happened, her gaze going to the puzzle box on the pedestal, and then looking back up at Ralph. "I'm not sure we have a choice in this."

"But—"

"We have to un-puzzle that box before tonight."

His eyebrows shot up, betraying the fact he never would have guessed that was what she would say.

She shrugged. "I'm not willing to risk Cybil's life,

but I also don't want the box to get into the wrong hands."

"Then let's go. Our hour showcase is up anyway."

She, Ralph, and Scott took the box back to the antique shop and to the backroom that Henrietta had transitioned into a meeting room she often rented out to book and writers' clubs and other small-member meetings.

They set it on the table and Ralph and Henrietta began to circle it, staring at it as if it might give up its secrets if corrected properly. Olivia was out front and Scott had gone to join her, but Henrietta had a feeling they would uncover the secret given the right thought process.

"Clearly he loved his granddaughter."

"How do you know that, though?"

"If what Cybil says is true, he did leave her his inheritance. Perhaps he learned not to let the sins of the mother be transferred to the daughter, but the moment she was born—"

"What?" Ralph said, resting his hands on the table.

"What if the numbers are a date? A date correlating to Cybil?"

"But how are we supposed to find that out? It's likely these cretins have the girl and are not going to let her go until this box is in their hands."

"True, but we can do a little creative math. It could be the year she was born. So, try 2000."

He moved the wheeled numbers to the right year, but nothing happened.

"All right. That leaves us…"

"Guess the month *and* the day. It will take all day and all night!"

"True," Henrietta wracked her brain for an answer. "Try…oh-three-oh-ten."

Ralph frowned then put in the numbers with a shrug. "Well, if we're making guesses, then I'll say—"

The box made a popping *click* sound and Ralph's eyes went wide. "How in tarnation did you know that?"

Henrietta smiled to herself. She wasn't one to hold things over anyone. As her mother said, *Pride makes no friends.* But this time, she was very glad her hunch had been right.

"Just pure detective work, Mister Gershwin."

"Care to enlighten?"

She grinned. "I remembered Cybil saying that her mother met a fisherman one *summer* and then she was sent away in the fall. I assume she would have had Cybil in either February, March, or April, depending. I picked March because it was central."

"But the tenth?"

"It was something else Cybil had said. She purchased her ticket to come out here on her lucky number—ten. Most people will use their birthday date for lucky numbers for some such reason. Seeing as how she'd had the best summer with her grandfather at the age of ten, I also decided to go with that. It seems I was correct."

"Amazing," Ralph said, and Henrietta had to remind herself not to be too proud of herself.

"What's in it?" she said, pulling herself back from back-patting.

"Uh…" He moved aside a little hinged door that was sprung open by the correct combination of the lock and extracted an odd key.

"Interesting," she said, taking it and inspecting it. "It could go to some part of the house. It looks like the right area for the Patton home."

"But how will we ever find out what it goes to?'

"Perhaps Cybil will have the answer to that."

"Does this mean you want to go through with the exchange?"

"I don't see that we have a choice."

"But it's not safe." He leveled his gaze on her.

"I'm afraid if we bring in the police, they'll spook, taking Cybil, and perhaps the box, with them."

Ralph considered this for a few minutes, then nodded slowly. "All right. We'll do the exchange, but—"

"No, *I'll* do the exchange"

"I'm not letting you go by yourself."

"Of course not," she said with a smile. "You'll be watching from nearby in case they don't hold up their end of the bargain. You can't trust thieves these days."

"I don't like the sound of this."

"Neither do I, but we really don't have a choice,

dear Ralph. I have a feeling we'll need Cybil to find what this key goes to, and with the box in the hands of whom I can only assume are Cybil's 'parents,' we can send the police after them to retrieve our stolen property."

He nodded slowly. "I can see where you're going with this. All right. But Scott is coming too."

"I agree. The more there—hidden in the grass along San Juan Point beach—the better chance we have of stepping in in case something goes wrong. But *only* if that is the case."

"You've got my word."

"Now, hand me that puzzle box," she said with a grin. "I've got an idea."

The night was cool. The breeze coming in from off the water wrapped around Henrietta like a chilly, wet blanket, and she was thankful for the windbreaker she had put on just before they left. It was by no means *cold,* but that didn't stop her from having goosebumps racing up her arms.

Henrietta stood on the beach facing the water. She knew that if she looked to her right, a few hundred yards and in the cover of dense bushes, she'd see Scott. Then, on the opposite side, if she searched the trees in that area, she'd likely be able to spot Ralph. Then again, he was very good at hiding.

She trusted he and his son not to interfere unless something was disastrously wrong, but she still wondered what would happen when everyone showed up and the exchange was going to take place.

Ralph and Scott had arrived almost two hours before the drop time, allowing for Henrietta to make an entrance in her own car—alone. She'd walked down, looking out at the water as the lights from across the way shone on it in a shimmering, distorted pattern.

The sound of tires crunching on gravel drew her attention back from the gravel to the parking lot. It was a county park that was almost never closed at sunset like the sign pronounced. Even if it had closed, no one would have pulled themselves away from the Blackberry Festival to do anything so mundane as close up a park for the night.

She tried to make out anything on the car but couldn't from her distance. She had a feeling that Ralph would be getting the license plate number with his high-powered binoculars, *if* he could see anything in the darkness.

She saw that three figures got out of the car, one clearly had her hands tied—likely Cybil—and then three sets of feet made their way down the narrow path toward the beach.

"Better have brought what we asked for," the man said. She was getting tired of not knowing their names but hopefully, she wouldn't have to deal with them for much longer after this.

"Yes. I brought it like you asked."

As they came closer, she saw that Cybil's mouth was taped and her eyes wide. Henrietta saw fear there—fear at her turning over the puzzle box. Did that mean she knew something about it?

"You can see we held up our end of the bargain." He shoved Cybil forward a little on the path.

Henrietta reached into the bag, and the man made a warning sound.

"Sorry," she said, holding out the bag. "I'm only getting the box. I promise."

"You'd better be telling the truth, lady."

Henrietta bristled at the woman's tone. She clearly had no regard or respect for her elders. "I do promise, *young* lady."

Then she pulled out the box. Its polished sheen was easily visible in the flashlight that the man held up. It slightly blinded her, but she looked away quickly to regain some of her night vision.

"Good. Now hand it over and—"

"I'd like you to take off the tape from Cybil's mouth, please."

The man scowled but finally reached up. She noted the slight bit of care that went in to him removing the tape and her theories were founded. It was Cybil's 'parents.' Though how any parent, step or otherwise, could do something like this to their daughter, she didn't know.

"Please, don't give them the box, Miss Henrietta."

"Hush, child," she said with a compassionate smile. "You and I both know that life is more important than any old box, secrets or not."

Cybil was about to protest when her stepfather put the tape back over her mouth. "Well?"

"We have a deal. I give you the box, you give me Cybil, and we both leave in peace."

Again, Cybil looked with terror between the box and Henrietta, but she closed her eyes as if she couldn't bear to see the box leave Henrietta's hands.

"On the count of three then," Henrietta said. "One, two..." She licked her lips. "Three."

The woman shoved Cybil forward, and Henrietta handed the box to the man. The next moment, they were backing up the pathway and then running to their car as Henrietta took the girl in her arms. "Hush now, dear. It's all right."

The sound of tires spinning on gravel floated down to them and Henrietta reached up to take the tape off Cybil's mouth. "There you are. Better?"

"You gave them the box," she said, tears streaming down her cheek. "My grandpa's puzzle box."

"Yes, dear, I did." She wiped the tears with a gentle thumb and met Cybil's gaze. "But not without getting the key first."

"The key? You have it?"

"I do." She smiled. "Do you happen to know what it's to?"

Cybil's countenance fell. "No, just that it's to something important."

"Henri, you okay down there?

Cybil jumped. "Who's that?"

"That is Ralph, and his son Scott is over there. We were never without safety."

Cybil began to cry at that moment, and Henrietta understood. It had no doubt been a very emotional day for her, being kidnapped by her stepfather and his wife, and now finding out that her grandfather's prized box was in the hands of criminals.

"But I promise you this, Cybil…" She gently squeezed the girl's shoulder. "We're going to find out what the key opens and how to prove you, in fact, *are* the rightful heir of Patton House."

13

Chesterton Mallory did not look at all pleased to see the young woman on the steps in front of him. He was even less pleased as Henrietta attempted to explain the young woman's claim to the heritage of Patton House.

"You must understand, Miss Hewitt..." He looked between her and Cybil. "Mister Patton *had* no heirs. That is, his daughter was the rightful heir, and then she died—"

"A year ago next Tuesday."

Chesterton started. "Um, that's right. How do you—"

"She was my mother. Cybil Patton."

Chesterton's eyes widened.

"Don't you see? They share the same name!"

"Aside from this young woman's claim that she is Cybil Patton, I have no evidence to that fact. She has no passport, no ID card, not even a driver's license. Besides, the new will is missing, so—"

"Missing?"

He bit his lip. "You didn't hear this from me, but Mister Patton did have a new will drawn up, but no one can find it."

Odd. Henrietta's eyes narrowed. "Surely there must be some sort of test she could take."

"Perhaps she could have taken a DNA test, but I'm afraid Mister Patton's ashes were scattered over the cliffs in the small ceremony following his death."

Cybil's eyes watered, and she tried to hide the tears.

"There has to be *some* way."

"Show me a birth certificate or social security card and then there might be grounds, but until then...she could just be an excellent fake."

Cybil's eyes blazed at his insinuation. "See that path?" She pointed to the foot path trailing along the side of the house. "It goes to the steep stairs that access the private beach. There is a squeaky board three steps up from the top on the central staircase. I spilled iced tea on the carpet in the sunroom." She burst into tears after this.

"I'm afraid anyone could know about the path, the stairs have been redone, and the carpet was replaced."

"Yes, of course."

"I'm sorry, but with the remodel of the house, a lot of what would have been true in the past is now covered up. Only memories are left."

"Yes, memories and—" Henrietta suddenly had a thought. "Thank you, Chesterton. We'll be back."

"I—" he stammered after them as she all but pulled Cybil down the steps toward her Mini Cooper.

"What is it, Henrietta?" she asked, wiping her eyes. She'd again spent the night with Henrietta, this time staying in her room until eight o'clock and leaving the normal way through the door. They had decided to try and see if there was a way around her not having any identification papers, but that hadn't turned out well.

Now, though, things might change.

"Do you have any photos of you as a child?"

Cybil scrunched up her nose in thought as Henrietta zoomed out onto the road. "I may have a TBT post on Instagram somewhere."

"A…a what?"

"Oh, sorry, a "throwback Thursday" post. It's a post that celebrates a memory or an older photo."

"I'm going to need you to find that. We're going to the library."

"All right," she said, pulling out her pay-by-the-minute phone. It had internet capabilities and she pulled up her Instagram, scrolling down as Henrietta schemed. There just might be a way to prove that Cybil was indeed Gerald Patton's granddaughter, but it would have to be via the 'old school' route.

They pulled into the parking lot, and Cybil let out an excited yelp. "How's this?"

"That should be perfect."

They rushed into the library and, after being directed to the right place, started digging. It took almost a half an hour but finally, Henrietta had what she had been hoping for: photographic evidence.

"Do you really think this will work?" Cybil asked.

"See," she said, holding up the photo she'd sent Cybil to print off and putting it side by side with the image she had uncovered. "This is your grandfather and *you* in front of the Patton house."

"But, it's still not hard proof. I mean, I could have just visited the house or something, you know? I'm just thinking of what that Mister Mallory guy will say."

"That would be true if it weren't for the article accompanying this image. It names you, Cybil Patton Markham, as the granddaughter to Gerald Patton."

Cybil raised her eyes to Henrietta. "Really?"

"Yes. Now, it is still not hard evidence per se. Your photo could have been doctored or such, but I feel like it should be enough to let us have a look at the will. Don't you?"

She shrugged. "I'd like to think so."

Just then, Henrietta's phone rang and she answered it to silence it, putting it to her ear as they left the library.

"What is it, Ralph?" She listened for a few moments then hung up.

"What was that about?" Cybil asked.

"That was Ralph, and it looks like the police may know where your stepparents are staying."

Cybil grimaced. "This is just becoming such a mess. I just wanted to come and see my grandfather, maybe help him, and get away from my life in New York. But now it's this big issue, and *they* are ruining it all." Tears pooled in her eyes and Henrietta clasped her hand, giving it a little squeeze.

"I know it's a lot to take in, but we have a few good things to take into account."

"What's that?"

"The fact you're safe. The fact we have the key. And the fact that I think you know what the key goes to."

Cybil's eyes widened, and she blushed. "How did you know?"

"Call it intuition." She directed them down the street, leaving her car in the library's parking lot. "Why don't we get some lunch and you can tell me all about it."

It took Cybil a few moments, but finally, she nodded. "I'd like to do that."

When they arrived at Henrietta's favorite deli, she could see that Cybil was shocked to find Ralph there waiting for them.

"Oh, hello. I didn't know you'd be there," she said, sliding into the booth seat.

"It was my suggestion."

Cybil's gaze traveled up to Henrietta's, eyes wide in

question. "I'm sorry, dear, but I had a feeling there were a few things you were keeping from us. While I *do* believe you are Gerald Patton's granddaughter and I *do* think you were trying to escape your stepparents, I don't think you are quite as ignorant of this whole situation as you've made yourself out to be."

Henrietta had taken up the seat next to her and Ralph was across the away so there was no chance that Cybil could escape, but Henrietta hoped that she would choose to stay.

The young woman took in a deep breath and then let it out slowly.

"Why don't I start you off with a question." Cybil's gaze turned to her. "Why did you try to buy the puzzle box at the auction?"

Cybil looked shocked. "How…?"

"It took me a while, but I realized that, when you came to this area, you did decide to stay in Sequim because you wanted to hide—understandable with your stepparents coming after you, but you also wanted to work at Frank's for two reasons. One, he was willing to pay you under the table, and two, you would be close to Patton House." Cybil didn't contradict her, so she continued. "I saw only your hand —covered in a black glove that I believe you left behind at your most recent job—at the auction, but considering the amount that you dropped out at, and a reasonable guess as to what you made at Frank's, I think I exceeded your allotted budget. I don't think you counted on anyone trying to outbid you. It was just a puzzle box anyway, right?"

Cybil nodded. "I highly doubted anyone would go over five hundred for a box. You proved me wrong."

"Yes, I did." Henrietta paused as their sandwiches were delivered. "The interesting thing was the fact that your stepparents then began to threaten me. I think they had contacted Ralph to find you but already knew the direction you were heading in. Ralph was likely more of a warning system—if he found you, then they would know you were close—but, then again, so were they."

"The thing that I don't understand," Ralph said, weighing in on the subject, "is what this whole key business is about. And how did your stepparents know about it?"

"I suppose this is the part of the story that I *can* fill in," Cybil said, taking a small bite of the dill pickle accompanying her sandwich before meeting Henrietta's gaze. "You're right, I do know more than I've let on. Before you judge me too quickly though, I wasn't sure who to trust."

"We understand. Go on."

"Remember I told you my mother got sick a year ago?" Henrietta nodded. "Well, on her deathbed, she shared with me a few things about our family I had never known. Like the existence of a safe that no one but she and my grandfather knew about. She told me the story of the puzzle box and how it was supposed to be her inheritance, but she would never see it."

"That's heartbreaking," Henrietta said quietly.

"I agree. It's the first time I'd heard of this. I mean, the last thing I knew of my grandfather after seeing him when I was ten was that he still disapproved of my mother's choices. Anyway, the night she told me about the key in the puzzle box, she also told me that she'd convinced my grandfather to put *me* in his will back all those years ago. I was shocked, but she said that it was right and he had agreed. It was only after I left that night that I saw my stepfather outside the room. I think he'd heard the whole conversation—or at least the last part of it."

Cybil took in a shuddering breath.

"What is it?" Ralph asked, picking up on her distress.

"Remember I said that my grandfather was sick?" They nodded in understanding. "Well, I don't think his death was an accident."

"What?" Ralph leaned forward even more.

"I confronted my stepfather and told him when I turned eighteen, I was out of there. That's when he started putting the lockdown on everything I did—including hiding my birth certificate. Instead, he met up with this woman—now his wife—and they began plotting. Or, at least I assume so. I think if you look into how my grandfather died and who was around him, she might pop up. It's a hunch and I have no evidence, but I think my stepfather heard my mother's comments about the wealth in the hidden safe and wanted to get into the house some way."

"But what good would it be if they didn't have the key?"

"That's just it. They thought they *were* getting the key when they exchanged me for the box."

Henrietta began to nod slowly. "So, your stepmother worked for your grandfather as what? A nurse or something?" Cybil nodded. "She gained entrance to the house and perhaps even found the safe, but then didn't have the key."

"Yes. I don't know if they realized the box would be auctioned. I only knew because I'd done some online research. Either way, they were busy looking for me while I was busy trying to get enough money to buy the box before they could get to it."

"Still," Ralph said around a bite of corned beef, "what do they think will happen? They'll just slip into the house, unlock the safe, and get away scot-free?"

"I'm not sure." Cybil picked at her chips. "I just know that the house and whatever is in that safe holds the key. Pun not intended." She shrugged.

Henrietta stared off into the distance. "I have a feeling that there is a little bit more going on here than what we are seeing."

Ralph and Cybil looked at her. "Why's that?"

"Intuition, my dear," she said to Cybil. "But the good thing about intuition is that it can always be proven—right or wrong."

14

Henrietta sat in the dark in the attic of Patton House, legs crossed. She was lost in thought when the sound of faint scratching reached her. Her lips curved into a small smile and she waited.

"This way," came the sound of a female voice.

"Are you sure?"

"You idiot. Of course I'm sure! I lived with the old geezer for four months, didn't I?"

"Right."

Then the sound of footsteps on the stairs came closer and Henrietta took in a deep but silent breath. When the sound reached the top of the stairs, she pulled the chain to the antique tiffany-style lamp and said, "Good evening."

The man and woman stumbled back, but not before Ralph stepped between them and the stairwell.

"What is this?" the man said. He had black hair and tanned skin with wrinkles next to his eyes.

"This," Henrietta said, "is what is known as a 'setup'." The man scowled. "But you know all about that, don't you, Mister Markham?"

His eyes widened, and she heard a gasp.

"What?" the woman said, looking between Henrietta and Paul.

"How—how did you know?"

"It took a while, but you left one clue that was unmistakable. The knot you tied me up with. A classic fisherman's knot. That and the quick nature of how Cybil's mother found and married you in New York as well as your relatively fair treatment of the girl made me think there was more to you than meets the eye. Cybil said you were a conman, and that's what this all felt like it was. A big con. You're not dangerous, but you are out for your own devices, aren't you?"

"So?" he said, looking around for an escape. "When life hands you lemons, you make lemonade."

"So, that means a few things," Henrietta said, easing into the explanation. "One is that you're more than a little familiar with this estate, and two, you have special reason to get into the safe first."

"Yeah? And why is that?" the woman asked. She was beginning to get on Henrietta's usually very patient nerves.

"Because I believe that you overheard your wife on

her deathbed saying that Gerald had changed the will. The will you *knew* had originally given everything to your wife and would, subsequently, go to you as her successor and guardian of her child.

"Then, when it became known that the new will was missing, it was your chance to get to it before anyone else. At present, the lawyers are going over the *old* will he had on file with his lawyer. The lawyer swears there was a new one but, without proof—since Gerald wanted to keep everything in his possession—it means nothing."

"How could you," Cybil said, stepping from the shadows.

"Oh, baby, I—"

"Don't." She shook her head and glared at the woman next to him. "And you. You *killed* my grandfather!" Cybil made to lunge at the woman, but Scott stepped out of his hiding place and held her back.

"I'd convinced your grandfather to put his important papers in it, but he did it when I was out shopping one day. Your father told me it was here somewhere, that he'd overheard your mom telling you about it, but when I finally found it, it was locked and there was no way to get in."

"You would betray me for money?" Cybil said, tears streaming down her face.

Her father hung his head. "I would never have hurt you," he said, and he sounded as if he was telling the truth. "I did send Valerie here to look for the safe but only to destroy the will if she found it. If everything went to *you*, then I knew you'd leave me in the dust. I couldn't let that happen."

"Why didn't you just tell me who you were?" She was still crying, sobs wracking her body.

"Because, in more ways than one, it was better for me to be your stepfather than your real one."

Cybil shook her head and slumped onto a dusty couch as police officers filed into the room from downstairs. They cuffed Mr. Markham and Valerie and took them out. When silence finally landed in the room, Henrietta turned to Cybil.

"Why don't you open the safe, dear girl. I think it's about time we see what Gerald Patton had in mind."

The tears had stopped and, as if in a dream, Cybil went to the wall with the poorly done still life painting on it. Pulling down the painting, she inserted the old-fashioned key into the lock. The safe door swung open to reveal a stack of papers.

She moved to the table where another light had been illuminated and dumped the papers. There, on the very top, was the most recently dated—and, until now, lost copy—of Gerald's will. Beneath it, Cybil saw a copy of her birth certificate, her father's name left blank, and then beneath that, an image of Cybil and Gerald on the front steps of the house.

"This was during that time I was here when I was ten," she said, wiping away more tears.

"Look," Henrietta pointed out. "He changed the will around the same time your mother was sick."

"I think he really did want to take care of me," she said. "And now, he's done just that.

With the puzzle box recovered and the confusion of the will amended, Henrietta sat behind the cash register, things having returned to normal in the antique shop. She was sad that the Blackberry Festival had ended, feeling like she'd missed most of it, but she was content as well. It really had been both the best and the most action-packed festival in her history.

She leaned back, regretting that all the unsold furniture was now back *in* the shop. She'd liked having an outdoor extension of her space. Something to consider for the rest of the summer, to be sure.

She also thought of Cybil. She'd asked the young woman to come by and, by the clock, that would happen any minute. It had been heart-wrenching to see a young woman estranged from her real father, not just her stepfather, but there was something to be said for knowing that her grandfather had cared for her enough to provide for her future. She would be well off if she decided to stay at Patton House or to sell it and move elsewhere.

The bells chimed at the front of the shop and a few moments later, Henrietta looked up to see Cybil come in followed by Ralph. "Saw this little lady walking and thought I'd give her a ride."

"I'm happy you could join us."

"I still need to get a proper license," Cybil said with a laugh. "But I'm working on it."

"I'm glad to hear that. I—"

The front door bells rang again, and they waited until Mayor Ricky Lawrence stepped into the room, a broad smile on his mouse-like face.

"Hello, hello!" he said brightly. "And what a surprising morning it is."

Henrietta merely smiled.

"What's so surprising about a Monday?" Ralph said. Henrietta wondered if he was still sore about the reality that he'd done all the work to find Cybil and would never be paid for it.

"I was just finishing up the silent auction bids when, to my surprise, I saw the winner of not only the largest auction bid, but also our most auspicious item. The puzzle box."

"What? Who was it?" Olivia said, coming out of the backroom where she'd been cataloging a new shipment of antique books.

"None other than our very own Henrietta Hewitt!" The mayor clapped his hands together and all eyes turned toward her.

"What?" she said, shrugging. Then she asked, "Olivia, will you get the box from the safe?"

"Of course."

When she came back out with it, Henrietta turned to Cybil. "I couldn't bear to see it fall into the hands of someone who wouldn't understand its significance or its secrets." She smiled and handed it to Cybil.

"Oh, thank you so much, Henrietta. I...I'm overwhelmed."

"As are we for your *generous* donation. I was thinking we could chat about next year's—"

"Here's your check," she said, interrupting the mayor, "and we'll talk come next summer. Okay?"

His eyes narrowed, and she knew he heard "the very beginning of next year" instead of the summer, but she'd take what she could get.

"Thank you, Henrietta."

He left, and Ralph stepped forward. "So, what's next for you, kiddo?"

She looked between the box, to Ralph, then to Henrietta. "Honestly, I'm not sure. I spoke with Mister Mallory and he's willing to stay on and help me a little with the managing of the estate. I don't really want to sell Patton House—at least not yet—so I'll stay, and who knows? Maybe do some traveling. Now that my father—" She cleared her throat. "Now that...*George* and Valerie are out of my life, I feel a new kind of freedom."

"I hope that you are able to discover all of what life offers but also to find good friendships with which to enjoy said offers." Henrietta patted the girl on the shoulder.

"Thank you. And I'd better be off. I have behind the wheel driver's training." She giggled like a schoolgirl. "Wish me luck."

"Maybe I'll stay here for a while. You know, off the roads," Ralph muttered as she left. Then he turned to Henrietta. "You bought the box? All that hoopla and *you* bought the box?"

"As I said, I think Cybil needed to have it. We found papers in the safe dictating that the box was to go to Cybil in the first place."

"That makes sense," Ralph said.

"As much as Cybil says that Valerie is to blame for her grandfather's death, I don't think she had a hand in it. I honestly think that Gerald passed away unexpectedly before he could fully arrange things. Like leaving papers out of the safe to ensure that the safe would be found." Henrietta offered a sad smile.

She was glad that things had wrapped up as they had, the pieces indeed falling into place, but it was also difficult to think that Cybil would never see her grandfather again and her already stilted relationship with her father had only worsened with the truth. Still, Cybil was better off away from the clutches of overbearing guardians. Somehow, she thought Cybil and Chesterton would make a good team when it came to Patton House.

"I've got to hand it to you, Henri. That was some detective work you did."

She shrugged. "I simply pulled the pieces together."

He let his gaze linger on her for longer than was comfortable, then offered up a roguish grin. "You sure I can't convince you to work with me?"

"I think you already have," she said with a grin.

Thanks for reading *Heirlooms and Homicide*. I hope you enjoy this new series. If you could take a minute and leave a review for me, that would be really appreciated.

The second story in the series is called *Break-ins and Bloodshed*. Henrietta finds herself involved in a string of robberies that turns into murder. Be sure to check it out today!

If you would like to know about future cozy mysteries by me and the other authors at Fairfield Publishing, make sure to sign up for our Cozy Mystery Newsletter. We will send you our FREE Cozy Mystery Starter Library just for signing up. All the details are on the next page.

FAIRFIELD COZY MYSTERY NEWSLETTER

Make sure you sign up for the Fairfield Cozy Mystery Newsletter so you can keep up with our latest releases. When you sign up, **we will send you our FREE Cozy Mystery Starter Library!**

FairfieldPublishing.com/cozy-newsletter/

Made in the USA
Coppell, TX
22 May 2020

26083029R00090